Rachel Dove is a tutor and romance/romcom author from West Yorkshire, in the UK. She lives with her husband and two sons, and dreams of a life where housework is done by fairies and she can have as many pets as she wants. When she is not writing or reading she can be found walking her American Cocker Oliver in the great outdoors, or dreaming of her next research trip away with the family.

Also by Rachel Dove

Fighting for the Trauma Doc's Heart

Discover more at millsandboon.co.uk.

THE PARAMEDIC'S SECRET SON

RACHEL DOVE

MILLS & BOON

First published in Great Britain 2021
by Mills & Boon, an imprint of HarperCollins*Publishers* Ltd,
1 London Bridge Street, London, SE1 9GF

www.harpercollins.co.uk

HarperCollins*Publishers*
1st Floor, Watermarque Building,
Ringsend Road, Dublin 4, Ireland

Large Print edition 2021

The Paramedic's Secret Son © 2021 Rachel Dove

ISBN: 978-0-263-28822-3

12/21

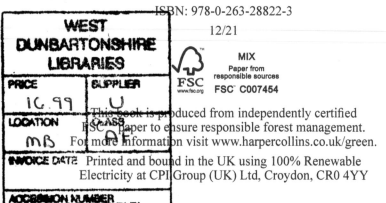

MIX
Paper from
responsible sources
FSC
www.fsc.org
FSC™ C007454

This book is produced from independently certified
FSC™ paper to ensure responsible forest management.
For more information visit www.harpercollins.co.uk/green.

Printed and bound in the UK using 100% Renewable
Electricity at CPI Group (UK) Ltd, Croydon, CR0 4YY

In memory of 'Aidy'—Adrian Rothwell.

Still dearly loved and missed by us all.

CHAPTER ONE

THE FIRST CALL came thirty-seven seconds into the early shift. A welcome distraction for Annabel, who had barely felt the coffee start to work after the morning she'd already had.

'Heathrow Airport, Terminal Two, fall after feeling faint. Incoming passenger from Finland, no history yet. Sixty-two-year-old male. Possible head injury from the fall.'

'Let's go.' Annabel grinned at her driving partner, turning on the sirens and strapping into the ambulance seat. 'I need to turn my crappy morning around. Saving a life might just do that.'

Tom, her long-running partner and work husband, pulled out of the ambulance station, Penny waving them off from the control desk as they pulled out into the slowly separating mid-morning traffic.

'Aidan?' he asked, flicking her a support-ive best friend look. Tom was a gem. She couldn't help but open up to him whenever they were together. She rolled her eyes at him now, puffing a strand of dark hair out of her way with a blow of exasperated air.

'Who else? The builders are leaving stuff everywhere; the whole gaff is covered in dust. He's fed up, poor kid. Plus, he's doing some big project at school, and he keeps leaving little bits of paper everywhere, and going through Mum's old photos. I feel like I'm constantly just cleaning up all the time, and it still looks exactly the same. I'm about ready to pack us both off to a hotel with a pool for the weekend, just to get some peace. I would have already, but the builders are bleeding me dry. I swear, I've been saving to buy our forever home for years, but now it's here I wish I'd realised how much work it was going to be.'

Tom kept his eyes on the road, ever vigi-lant, but chuckled. 'It's your dream though! Just imagine what it's going to be like when it's all done. What's up with the little man, anyway?'

'Lord knows. Early hormones maybe? He's so moody lately,' she carried on, mentally checking the rig and the traffic as she talked about her frustration. They were going to be at the call soon, and then it would be all business.

Aidan was doing a project about family. She didn't tell Tom this, but she was pretty sure that the lack of names on Aidan's family tree had a little something to do with his current mood.

'It turned into a whole thing this morning. Apparently, I'm an utter dork and he hates living in the new house. I figured he'd forget about it a little once I'd explained that the work wouldn't take forever. And that I wasn't a dork. Obviously.'

'Obviously,' Tom chortled. 'Then what?'

'Then I dropped him off at breakfast club and…*ugh*. It was just tense, and I hate waving him off like that. He's not my biggest fan today.'

The station radioed, asking for an updated

ETA, and Annabel got to work, flashing him a rueful smile. She saw him clench his jaw, but he said nothing else, just put his foot down as soon as the traffic opened up.

'Nothing to say?' she probed once the cab fell silent once more, the sirens the only noise around them. Tom raised his brows, but still said nothing. Annabel huffed at him, but he smirked and ignored her. 'He is your godson.'

'Yep, and I'm not going to get involved. He still likes me.' Annabel's resulting scowl made him guffaw with laughter. 'Just cut him some slack. I know he's testing your limits, but it must be a lot for him too, right? It's not been the easiest of years for either of you. With his fall, and your big move? He's lived in one place his whole life, and so have you. It must be hard leaving your mother's flat; it's a connection to her that you've needed since she passed. I remember how upset you were when you started training. Your mother died, you started training to be a paramedic, then Har— Aidan came along. You haven't taken your foot off the accelerator for a long time.

Once you get your house done, you need to enjoy life a little more, that's all.'

She huffed again, crossing her arms, but she knew he was right. It had been a busy time, and she knew how changes could affect a person better than most. She thought back to Aidan's fall. She'd been on shift when the call had come through from Aidan's school. He'd had a bad fall from the equipment in the gym. She hadn't taken the call, but she'd rushed straight to hospital as quickly as she could, to be by his side. Just thinking of her little boy, unconscious and covered in wires and tubes, it still made her shudder. Life could change in an instant. She owed it to both of them to relax a little, start to enjoy the little things a bit more.

'I know; you're right. This year has taught me to cherish the everyday a bit more. Aidan's probably picking up on my stress too.' She looked across at her friend, playfully tapping him on the arm. 'You're going to be a great dad, you know.'

Tom kept his eyes on the road but his face lit up.

'Oh, I know. Watching you all these years, I picked up a thing or two. We can't wait.'

'Another lamb to the slaughter,' Annabel muttered. 'I can't wait to see it either. I might even buy popcorn.'

They pulled into the airport in record time, heading for Terminal Two and their casualty. A small crowd of people were surrounding a shuttle bus pulled over at the side of the road, and Annabel pointed Tom their way. A couple of people from the crowd heard them coming and started to flag them down.

'Oh, thank goodness!' An ashen-faced woman wearing a bright floral summer dress half pulled Annabel out of the cab. 'It's my husband! He needs to go to hospital!'

Annabel felt the woman's shaky hand encase her gloved one, and she squeezed it gently. 'We're here to help, but I have to get my equipment quickly. I need my hand, okay?' She stressed that last part, knowing that the seconds were ticking away. The woman smiled through her panic and let her go. Within seconds, they were by the patient's side, but someone was already working on the man lying on the ground, a beach towel underneath him that cushioned him from the harsh surface beneath him.

'Sir, could you step aside, please?' Tom asked the man. 'Help's h—'

Annabel's gasp cut Tom off. Either that, or she didn't hear anything he said after her shock discovery. Her world had tilted sideways for a second, but she found she was still on her feet. She was suddenly years younger, sitting back on that airport bench, with waffle marks on her behind from the metal bench. And a broken, utterly shattered heart as she watched the man she loved walk out of her life forever. Her stomach recoiled at the memory.

Please, please, don't let me vomit in this damn airport again because of this man. It can't be him. She blinked hard. *I'm seeing things. What the heck was in that coffee?*

There was a man crouched over the patient, who was conscious and seemingly looking for someone, his head moving from side to side. His hands were reaching for someone as the man tried to settle him, speaking softly to him and trying to keep him from getting up. The wife pushed past the two ambulance personnel and knelt by his side. Tom started to talk to the Good Samaritan, asking curtly for details of what had happened, and Annabel walked towards the patient. Luckily, the professional part of her brain had switched to autopilot and she was focused on the job. The rest of her was in utter shock and wanted to turn the heck around and run for the hills. She knew she needed to run to the patient but her legs were uncooperative blobs of jelly. Just putting one floppy foot in front of the other was a herculean effort. All she could think about was the look on the Samaritan's face when he saw her: the look of utter disbelief at what he was seeing. She wondered what the expression on her own face might have told him. Did she look just as shocked as she felt?

He always could read me. It seems that some things never change. I need to focus! The patient. Dear God, why is he here now?

Is it a coincidence? I need to work. Focus on work. I've wasted enough years wondering about what's going through that man's head, let alone his motivations. Get the job done and get the heck out of Dodge. It doesn't matter what he's doing here, as long as he's going. Maybe he's here to fly off again—he's good at that.

She took her chance as Tom distracted the man, to get to the patient lying on the floor.

She checked the vitals of the patient, talking to the man she now knew to be Frank Jessop, returning from a very busy holiday visiting family who'd moved to Finland. He'd overindulged on the flight, it seemed, and had a dip in blood pressure that sent his heart into overdrive. Lugging cases and sitting on a cramped, hot shuttle bus had been the last straw. Hitting the bus rail on the way down, he now had a fall to add to his misery.

Checking him over, Annabel was satisfied he had no obvious broken bones, but the pain in his back and knock to the head meant he needed to be transported safely to hospital to be checked over fully. His vitals were stable and holding steady. No blown pupils, and he tracked her finger with no issues. He had a headache, but nothing too concerning. He would be fine, but still needed to have a trip to hospital.

Now brought around by his Good Samaritan, however, Frank was eager to get up off the floor and on his way home. He was embarrassed and eager to forget about the whole thing. Annabel knew how he felt as she crouched down next to him on the ground. She could see that Tom was dealing with the small crowd, getting people on their way on the shuttle bus. Keeping *him* at arm's length from her, which she was grateful for.

Thank goodness she was working with Tom and not one of the others. The conversation Tom would want to have was going to be bad enough. She didn't want the rumour mill to start up again; she couldn't bear it. Especially not in her current role. She was the lead paramedic now; she didn't want to be the subject of whispers and awkward looks in the corridors again any time soon.

* * *

'I'm sorry, Frank, but we do need to take you in, get you checked over properly. You can't drive home, but you can make arrangements with your family to collect your car. Okay?' She could see the panic creep back onto the man's face, and she smiled at him gently. She had sounded a little robotic. She licked her lips, suddenly feeling parched. Exposed to the rays of the hot sun, and her own past. She kept her eyes focused on her patient's face.

'Don't worry, the car parking company have plans for this kind of thing. They'll get it all arranged till you can collect your car. Let's get you sorted, okay? My colleague will bring the stretcher.' She looked across to Tom, but he was already on his way over with the equipment they needed. The Samaritan was standing off to one side, near to Frank's wife. *How caring of him,* she thought childishly. She didn't look at the man as they got Frank strapped in and wrapped up, but she felt as if his eyes were boring into her cheek the whole time.

'Annabel?'

Hearing him say her name felt like an arrow right through the heart. How long had it been since she'd heard him speak her name? How many times had she spoken his, on the messages she'd left on his phone? The ones he had never answered. *'I'm sorry, Annie,'* were the last words he'd spoken to her, before walking through the security doors and leaving her standing there, in this very airport.

'Annie?' He said it again now, a little louder. She ignored him, but her whole body flinched, and she really had to stop her head from turning to the sound.

'Annabel,' he tried again. 'Please...'

'I'm working, sir,' she said as coldly as she could. She heard the break in her voice and hated herself for it. *Suck it up, Annie!* 'If you could just stand back and let us do our work.'

'I was first on scene...' he started, but she cut him off. She wouldn't compromise the patient, and she had done a thorough check-up on Frank. She and Tom had this, and she didn't want to be in *his* proximity a minute longer than she had to be. She felt as if her whole body were on fire, and she didn't like how out of control she felt.

'Thank you for that. If you have any pertinent information, my colleague can take it.' She risked looking at him now and felt so grateful that she'd managed to arrange her face into a professional, emotionless expression. It was one of the hardest things she'd ever done. Last week she'd abseiled halfway down a building to reach a casualty who was locked out on a balcony and unconscious. Thinking about it, that had actually been far easier than looking Harrison—Harry— Carter straight in the face without either breaking down, punching him right in his stupid girlfriend-abandoning face or running into his arms. She couldn't deal with him right now, or ever. She thought about the last time she had uttered his name, and she felt her cheeks flush at the memory.

He can't be here because of that though, right? If he is, he's a bit late. Six months late. Eight years late, for that matter. He's had plenty of chances to come back, and he's never taken any of them before.

She found herself staring deep into his eyes despite herself, trying to read him.

God, if only the frontiers of medicine could crack mind-reading. It would mean a lot fewer broken hearts. She wanted to know just what was going on in that beautiful head of his. His stupid, woman-leaving head.

'Why are you here?' she blurted, just as Tom arrived with the stretcher.

'I came to see you,' Harry said simply, and as Annabel's emotions did a double-take she felt Tom touch her arm, bringing her back to reality.

'You ready?' Tom was looking at Harry with a wary expression, as if he were waiting for him to explode and take the lot of them out with him. 'Annabel?'

'Yep, yep!' she yipped back like an overexcited terrier, turning away and looking at Tom. He nodded to her once before glaring back at Harry.

'You okay?' Tom said out of the corner of

his mouth as they got the equipment ready. 'Did he really just say he'd come to see you?'

Out of the corner of her mouth, she shushed him.

'Tom! He'll hear you! And yes.'

'I can hear you just fine, dear,' Frank said as they lifted him off the ground. 'My hearing's fine. I really think I should just go home. I don't need all this fuss. You should be looking after someone who's sick.'

'Sorry, Frank you have a ride in the ambulance ahead of you. We need to get you checked over.'

Frank tutted, and Harry stepped forward. 'Can I help?'

'No,' Annabel said bluntly. 'Please, just step back and let us do our job.' She gave him a look that meant to maim. 'We don't need you here.' Harry raised his arms in surrender, his face a picture of hurt as he stepped back away from them. Annabel winced inwardly, but then thought back to being in that airport as her boyfriend told her he was going away without her, and her resolve strengthened.

Securing Frank to the gurney now, Annabel kept her head focused on the job. She just couldn't look at her friend. *Their friend, once upon a time.* One look right now at Tom and he would read her face and know her truth. She felt as if her secret was radiating out of her, and Tom had been suspicious enough over the years. One look, and he would work it out. She couldn't let that happen, especially with *him* right here. He was standing back from the small crowd now, alone, a suitcase at his feet.

Great. Anything else you want to throw at me today? A swarm of locusts, maybe?

She took him in once more as they pushed Frank to the ambulance, his wife following close behind, Tom talking to Frank, keeping a close eye on his vitals. She was looking at the details too—Frank, Tom and his attempts to catch her eye, and him. Harry. The man she'd once declared to be the love of her life. The one she'd also claimed, to everyone she knew, to be dead to her. He didn't look dead, of course. He looked positively glowing in fact. Tanned, well dressed, a little tired per- haps. She hoped that jet lag would bite him on the behind. He was due a bit of karma, surely? He was bronzed, his hair even lighter than she'd remembered. His sun-kissed skin was a perk of his fancy job, no doubt. Life must have been good in Dubai.

Well, la-di-dah. Good for you, Harry. Your new life without me obviously agrees with you.

He looked less of a boy now, of course, but she could still see him there underneath the day's worth of dark stubble. The angular jaw he kept flexing, tight-lipped as he looked right back at her. She saw that his legs were still strong and muscular, thicker set now than when she'd lain beside him, her limbs entwined with his. He still had the slightly floppy look to his blond hair, the nervous little twitch in the corner of his mouth. They got closer to him, and she watched as he collected his case and walked towards the car park. He didn't look back once. She swallowed to stop herself from calling his name impulsively. All she could hear in her head was his voice. *I came to see you.*

Looking back at Tom, she finally met his

eye. They had a bit of a code, honed over the years of working together. It had been eight years since Harry had left, and Tom knew what seeing him again would do to her. He nodded once at her, their shorthand for checking the other was okay. She nodded back, her usual 'I'm fine' nod. Tom frowned but turned his focus fully back to the job. Reaching behind him for the door, he opened up the back and they got back to work. Before Annabel closed the ambulance double doors she looked around, but Harry was gone.

'As if I could ever expect anything else,' she muttered under her breath, before swinging the metal doors shut once more against her old, long thought buried pain.

Tom was the best friend a woman could ever ask for. He really was. Married to the job, and restaurant owner Lloyd, he was the ultimate paramedic partner. Not to mention the fact that he and Lloyd had taken her on some of the best nights out she'd ever had, they were great with their godson Aidan and they always, always had her back.

The week that Harry had left, the pair of them had declared him a scoundrel and vowed never to talk to him again. And they hadn't. No one had, truth be told. Not that Annabel had ever asked that of anyone. She'd pushed the other way even, in the early days. The truth was that for the first three weeks she'd wanted them to get in touch with him. She'd called him more than a few times, even called the hospital in Dubai he was supposed to be working in. All she'd got was a wall of silence. She'd wanted to know he was okay, as much as she'd hated herself for it. She wouldn't give him the satisfaction of begging him to come home or talk about how heartbroken she was without him, but it didn't mean that she could just turn her feelings off. As much as she'd tried to.

She'd been in shock for the longest time when he'd left. In the back of her mind she'd even hoped he would come back to her on his own. Get over there and miss her, realise he was still in love and come to get her back by his side. Hear one of her voicemails or read one of her texts and realise what he was doing.

But there'd been nothing, and she hadn't called him since those first few weeks after he'd left. She couldn't, not once she'd realised that he wasn't going to call back or come home and she would have to deal with everything he had left behind all alone. She'd vowed to herself that from then on she would never contact him again, and she'd stuck to it for years. Almost perfectly, till one day six months ago. Now look what had happened. He'd been there, in that airport of all places. Like the Ghost of Christmas Past, complete with sun-kissed skin and a look in his eyes she'd never seen before.

He'd looked so unruffled by seeing her, but he'd said he'd come to see her. What did he want? Why now? Had he been talking to someone in her life? Surely he hadn't hopped on a plane just to tell her that he still wasn't bothered about her. What she knew now, after seeing him, was that she was still bothered by him. When she'd passed by him she'd felt as if she was on fire. She'd wanted to talk to him even, hear what he had to say…but she didn't even want to know what he would say. It was too risky, and things were complicated enough. Would he still want to talk to her if he knew all the facts? Did he know all the facts?

All of these questions were making her head spin, and for the millionth time in the last eight years she doubted the decisions she had made since he'd left. She couldn't take them back now, and she wasn't ready to deal with them either. Burying her head in the sand had served her well up to now, or so she'd thought. The second she'd set eyes on Harry, her blood had turned to ice in her veins.

What had she done? What if he hated her?

For the longest time she'd felt as though she hated him, but the thought of him despising her knocked her off her feet even now.

Oh, heavens, it was pointless anyway. The whole thing was a mess, and now her morning was utterly ruined. She sighed and took a seat next to Frank's wife Janice, in the back.

'Ready, Tom,' she called and half a second

later the vehicle was on the move, sirens on. Janice whimpered at the side of Annabel, and she put her hand on hers.

'Don't worry; it's just to get you there quicker. Traffic is a nightmare here this time of day.'

Janice nodded, the worry still evident on her face. 'Thank you. My daughter's on the way to pick the car up and the cases, so that's something. I do wish we hadn't troubled you. You must be so busy.'

Annabel waved her away, keen to help her feel settled in such a scary situation. 'No trouble at all. It's what we're here for. How long have you two been married?'

'Coming up to forty years now,' Frank replied, reaching for his wife with a shaky hand. 'It's why we went away, a little trip to see some family that moved abroad. My brother and his wife and their kids. We had such a lovely time, and now look.'

'Don't worry, you'll be fine, Frank. Don't let this spoil the memories of your trip. You got a lot of family?'

Janice reached into her handbag and pulled

out a little book of photos. On the front cover, it read *Grandparents Brag Book*. 'Oh, yes! We have seven grandchildren, and our first great-grandchild on the way. Plus our two daughters.' She flipped through the book, and Annabel saw the pride on her face as she looked at each memory. People with smiling faces, babies sleeping in bouncers, birthday parties full of life and obvious love. 'You got any kids?'

'One,' she said. 'Aidan.' She reached into her pocket, unlocking the screen on her phone to show them both a photo of her son. He was dressed in his school uniform, standing in front of the front door of their old flat, beaming smile and book bag in hand. 'He's in primary school.'

'He's lovely.' Janice leaned in close to the screen. 'He looks like you.'

'I get that a lot.' Annabel smiled, checking on Frank as they chatted. 'It's just the two of us, so we're pretty close. He's a little whirlwind, keeps me on my toes.'

'He looks like butter wouldn't melt,' Frank muttered, wincing when he turned his head.

'Good age, by the looks. Enjoy it before the hormones kick in.'

Janice laughed. 'Oh, yes, wait till puberty hits. With our girls, I think we aged about ten years overnight.'

Frank groaned theatrically, and the two of them gave each other a knowing look. 'I used to beg my boss for overtime; it was easier than dealing with the moody twosome at home.'

Thinking about Aidan that morning, Annabel could relate. 'Kids, eh?' she laughed. 'Can't live with them, can't live without them.'

'Grandkids make up for it though. Plus, seeing your kids get a taste of their own medicine has given us a few laughs over the years. Best of all, you get to hand them back at the end of the day. You have any other family?'

She thought of her mother, feeling the familiar pang of loss stab at her, and nodded slowly. 'I have people in my corner. It takes a village, right?'

She thought of her station family, and the man at the airport. *He was my family once.*

'We do okay; it's always been just us. He

has everything he needs.' She didn't know who she was trying to convince, but she squashed down the maelstrom of feelings pulsating through her.

We're just fine. Aren't we?

'How do you know the man who helped us?' Janice asked innocently. 'I saw you talking to him. We'd like to thank him too, if we could.'

It was said so innocently, but Annabel couldn't bring herself to answer at first. Quantifying Harry into a single sentence was impossible, but she tried anyway.

'I knew him a long time ago. Since the first year of primary school, actually. He moved away after we qualified; he used to be one of us.'

Janice nodded, seemingly satisfied. 'Are you still in touch? Could you thank him for us?'

She still had his number in her phone, despite having changed handsets over the years. It was a weakness of hers, so she pushed down the whirl of emotions running through her and gave Janice's hand a pat.

'I will,' she lied easily. 'I'll let him know.' One more thing to never tell Harry to add to the list. At least this one was small in comparison to the others.

'Annabel, are you going to talk about this, or are we going to be silent the whole shift?' In response, Annabel took a huge bite of her sandwich. Tom shook his head, taking a swig of his take-away coffee. They were sitting in the ambulance, having their break whilst parked in the grounds of the local community centre.

It was pretty quiet today, most of the classes and groups already having taken place earlier in the day. She'd been to a few of them herself over the years. Baby massage classes with Aidan, helping out at the coffee mornings to raise funds for new equipment. She'd even taught a few first aid courses here, helping out the centre by donating her time and expertise. There was a lot of social inequality in the area, and Annabel had seen enough of it to know that real change happened right at the root. It had helped her, back when she was still managing being a new single mum and keeping her career going. The memory made her smile, but she turned it off quickly. Tom was still staring at her as if she were a zoo exhibit.

'Stop staring, Tom, I'm fine. He's an ex; I was bound to see him some time. They don't go off and live on some remote island, you know. They do live on.'

'More's the pity,' Tom added. 'But this isn't just some ex; this is Harry. He also lives in another country, so seeing him again is not like bumping into him at the supermarket. And he isn't just some ex either; he's *the* ex. Wanting to talk to you. Harry. You know, your childhood sweetheart Harry. The man who left you alone to live a luxurious life in the opulence of the Middle East Harry. The man who broke your—'

'Trust in men—yeah, I got it. I don't want to talk to him. Whatever he has to say won't be good. He did me a favour, anyway. Jetting off to a dream paramedic job living in Dubai is all well and good, but I didn't even have a job to go to over there; I was just following him to his. I might not have even found a job, and then where would I have been? Sitting alone in some fancy place on my own while he carved out a career? I wouldn't have gone to work at the station or got my dream job with you guys. Looking back, it was all a huge gamble really. I didn't have a firm plan, and I worked hard to be a paramedic. It all worked out for the best.'

Wow, Annabel, that almost sounded like you believe your own fibs. You would have followed that man to the ends of the earth, and you know it.

Tom gave her a long sideways look before taking a bite of his own lunch. In between mouthfuls, he kept on at her. 'You would have landed a job in Dubai, and you know it. You're amazing at what you do. Not to contradict you either, but you trusted one man, remember? Long enough to make Aidan anyway. You could do it again, and Aidan won't be living at home for ever. You deserve to be happy, Annabel. Put the Harry thing to rest, finally. If he really is home to speak to you, hear him out.'

Annabel swallowed the piece of chicken from her wrap carefully before answering.

'No, I don't want to hear a word of what he has to say. And yes, I had a drunken one-night stand one time, after Harry left, and now I'm a single mum and—' She raised her finger at him when he tried to cut in. 'And I am happy with my lot. I don't want Harry to know about my life, and I mean any part of my life. I have the house now, and Aidan to raise. I don't need to see Harry to be reminded of that.'

He'd had his chance. Eight years ago, and six months ago. He'd failed both times. When she'd seen him at the airport he had full use of his limbs. He could quite easily have picked up the phone, or even a pen to send a blinking postcard. *Leave me alone. Stop calling. I left you for someone else. I'm married. I'm the new James Bond.* Anything would have been better than nothing, than wondering what it was about her that had made him fall out of love and leave her sobbing in the departure lounge while he strode away from her, ready to fly away to a flash new life.

She heard Tom sigh at the side of her, a sure sign that he was holding his tongue and resenting the notion. They'd been here many times over the years, but Tom had never crossed the line. He respected her wishes, even though he didn't always agree with them.

She wound her window down, eager to feel the hot city sun on her face. 'I'm happy, Tom. I promise. Hear that, universe?' she half shouted out of the window. 'I'm happy, thanks, you can send him back now!'

Tom chortled beside her. 'Of course you are, you lunatic. But with your mum being… gone, and that big house to sort out, don't you think it might be nice to have another pair of hands around the place? I know you're used to looking after yourself by now, but it doesn't mean you have to.'

Annabel ripped into her wrap again with gusto, the adrenalin and shocks of the morning making her feel ravenous.

'My mum died when I was eighteen, Tom. Before I even started training. I've looked after myself for a long time now, and her for that matter. She was sick for a long time before the cancer finally took her. Besides, I have another pair of hands around the place. Abe's been helping out at the weekends, keeping Aidan occupied, and I've got some contractors doing the bulk of the work.' Tom raised his brows pointedly, and Annabel slapped her forehead when recognition hit. 'Oh, no—Abe! Do you think he knows? About Harry being back?'

Tom shrugged. 'I don't know, but Abe's his dad and he stopped talking to him too. Maybe Harry wants to make amends with more than just you. Do you think Abe would talk to him? Harry must be staying somewhere, right? Do you think he'd go to his dad's?'

Annabel sank into her seat. She'd never even thought of that.

'I don't know. When Harry chose to be a paramedic and not train to be a GP, Abe took it badly. They fought for years, and when Harry told him we were both leaving for Dubai, they had a huge fight. Abe's been my rock ever since, but Harry's his flesh and blood. I wouldn't want him to choose between his son and me. I'll give him a call later, try and suss out if he knows anything,' she said glumly.

Tom squeezed her shoulder. 'Don't worry; he's probably just visiting. He's got a life in Dubai, right? A job to go back to. Seeing him there at the airport was bad timing, sure, but he's officially come with a purpose. I'm sure he'll fly off again soon, once he's said his piece.'

Looking out of the window, she felt her head nod, but inside all she could think was how the thought of Harry leaving London again gave her a punch in her gut that she wasn't expecting to feel, and she knew that it wasn't going to be that easy. Not at all. God, she wished her mother were still here, so she could talk to her. Ask her what she thought.

It wasn't as if she hadn't said plenty when she was alive. Her mother being taken by cancer had robbed her of all those conversations. Something told her that things weren't going to be easy, and she felt a fresh wave of grief that she couldn't run to her mother, the one person who knew everything about her and Harry growing up, and always supported her. Even though her comments sometimes had stung a little. That was mothers though; they always wanted the best for their babies, and had strong opinions when they didn't agree with their offspring's life decisions. Her mother had been no different, but she would give anything to have her here right now, even if it was just to give her a swift kick on the behind. She wondered again what her mother would have made of Harry leaving her like that. How much she would have loved Aidan and being a grandmother. She hoped that, wherever she was, she was proud of them both.

As they finished their lunch and greened up their console indicating their ability to take a shout, ready for the rest of the shift, she packed up the rubbish. And her emotions. It was time to be a paramedic again. She focused on that. The rest would have to wait. It would all just have to wait.

Harry could hear his heartbeat pulsate like a jungle drum in his ears as he walked away from the scene, from Annabel. She'd taken his breath away, standing there. She was just like he'd imagined, bar the scowl and tired eyes. The look on her face when she'd seen him. The way she'd shut down his attempts to talk. He'd played this moment over in his head so many times over the years. The fact that their first meeting had happened at the airport was awful. The place where he'd left her alone and jetted off to his new life.

He could still remember the confusion on her face that day. She'd met him at the airport, bags packed, all ready to come with him to their new life abroad. The look on her face when he told her he'd cancelled her plane ticket, that it wasn't working out. That he wanted to go alone, and wanted her to stay back in London, start over without him. He'd known this girl since they were snot-nosed kids in primary school, playing tag and growing up together. They'd gone through school together, trained together; their parents had been friends. He'd thought he was going to spend the rest of his life with her, but it wasn't to be and he'd ended up breaking her heart.

The one thing he never thought he'd do. He'd been so excited and terrified to see her again, but seeing her there at the airport, tending to Frank, was the worst possible moment.

It was the last place he'd wanted to see her again. And he knew he would see her again and make her listen. He'd come this far, had waited so long to make his move, and he wasn't about to stop now. He'd hidden long enough, and he hated himself for being such a coward for so long. The younger Harry who had left her had been like a scared little boy, reeling from his own problems and not wanting to drag her along with it. Not after everything she had already been through. He was the one who was supposed to bring her joy, not sorrow.

Looking back, he wondered whether that was the right decision. He'd questioned it every day since. People had tried to get in touch with him. His friends, his father, and Annabel. He'd never replied to a single one, had deleted the text messages as soon as they came through. He couldn't bear to listen to the voicemails. They would only be full of anger and hurt anyway. The ones from Annabel he never read or listened to. He knew that if he heard her voice he would come undone and he just couldn't do that. He'd chosen his path and, as hard as it was, he had thought it easier in the long run. On her, if not both of them.

Moving home after eight and a bit years was never going to be easy, but he'd come with a purpose. To finally right the wrongs of the past and put down roots. He'd not announced to anyone that he was coming, and when Frank fell to the floor on that shuttle bus he'd acted instinctively. It hadn't even occurred to him that Annabel might be in the ambulance coming to help. And with Tom as her partner. You couldn't make it up, how odd life was.

Tom was their friend, back in the old days. They'd all gone through training together. Tom had been cool towards him too, but he expected nothing else, and Harry could tell that his shock had given way to wanting to protect Annabel, and he couldn't begrudge him for that. Tom was a good friend, and

Harry had walked out on him too, in a way. Another person who'd called to check on him and got ignored. He'd dropped out of his life and never been back. Out of all their lives.

And now he had to go see his dad and tell him the good news. The prodigal son was home. Well, not home. He was going to book into a hotel. He wasn't that stupid. Once he got settled, he'd find somewhere more permanent. The fight they'd had before he'd left for Dubai was the last time they'd seen each other face to face, and he steeled himself for looking his dad in the face again. Abe had told him he was a disappointment years ago, and he didn't expect him to feel any differently now. Whatever Harry did to try to live his life and not hurt others, it never seemed to work out quite right. He hoped that now he was back in London he could break that curse. His thoughts led him to think of Annabel once more.

She'd looked at him as if he were a stranger. Less than a stranger. She'd looked at him with pure horror showing as plain as day on her features. He didn't expect anything less, of course, especially given the setting of their reunion. Harry knew that must have been brutal, and it was all down to him. He wished he could have told her that, that he was sorry she'd seen him there. Another Annabel conversation to torture himself with. Great. As if he didn't have enough of those already. Heading to the huts representing the numerous hire car companies, he steeled himself. London, Harrison Carter is coming home. I hope you're ready for this one.

Annabel drove the ambulance back into the station. They'd finished on time for once, and she and Tom were eager to get on with the rest of their day. Well, Tom was looking forward to a hot shower and a cold drink in a fancy wine bar with Lloyd. Annabel was looking forward to catching up on paperwork before picking Aidan up from his friend Finn's house. They'd had coding club after school, and then Finn's mum, Teri, was taking them out for tea. Teri was a nurse and the two single women had soon worked out that since their boys were such good friends, they could trade off on the childcare from time to time. It worked out brilliantly, and they got on great at work too. It made the two women's lives that much easier, and they always had each other's backs at work too.

Annabel frowned to herself when she thought of picking Aidan up from hers that night. How many lies she would have to tell—how much she would have to conceal about her day. Suddenly thankful for the list of jobs that needed her attention, she started to grab her things and head indoors to her office. Being the lead paramedic was great; it was what she had planned for her career for so long, and the bump in money was pretty nice too. Since things with Harry and moving to Dubai had fallen apart, taking the job she'd been offered at her old hospital—but had turned down in favour of Dubai—had made perfect sense.

Abe, Harry's dad, had held her together for the first few weeks, when she couldn't bear to go straight back to her flat with her tail between her legs to stare at four walls and wail. Thank goodness she'd not sold it before the planned move, or she would have been home-less to boot. Abe had even called the hospi-tal, let the others know what had happened, and that she was tragically single and avail-able for work. Dumped at the airport. She'd rocked up, cases in hand at Heathrow, and instead she had been dumped.

I'm going alone. It's not you, it's me. It would never work out there. Smell you later.

Everyone knew she'd got dumped by Harry and left to rot in her old life. Not that she saw it that way now. Things happened for a reason, and she knew that better than most. What had happened after, having Aidan, had kept her hands pretty full. She loved her job, had friends, a new home. She had been doing just fine, or she thought she had till she'd looked at Harry again. Felt the pull of him right in the pit of her stomach, just as strongly as before. Now she was back to feeling tired and wanting to hide away.

Heading into the ambulance station, she nodded to a few of the staff and motioned to-wards her office with a smile and a nod when they offered her some supper. She knew she probably should eat something, but she also knew that she'd only end up ordering pizza once Aidan was asleep in bed. She'd have the energy for little else.

Wading through her inbox, she noticed a new staff member form. Of course—Tom's replacement. They'd do a handover, and Tom would be gone. Off to pastures new, baby vomit and lack of sleep. If anyone could handle that, it was Tom. She was thrilled for both of them and couldn't wait to meet the new arrivals. Even if the little ones, not yet born, were the reason that she was losing the best work partner she'd ever had. Well, the second best. The pair of them were on standby, adoption process all done. They were just waiting for the call that the mother had delivered and they were parents.

She pulled out the staff form and laughed to herself softly. She was seeing things now. Imagining her ex's name in the square marked 'Employee Name'.

Rubbing at her tired eyes, she looked again. Blinked a half dozen times. It wasn't an optical illusion. A Mr Harrison Abraham Carter was due to start as her partner the very next day.

The words swam in front of her eyes as she slotted the pieces together. HR had hired a new paramedic, and they'd told her that he was a previous employee. She'd never connected the dots. She'd never ever imagined that Harrison would even be in the UK, let alone in their neck of the woods. She'd stayed hands off, not wanting to seem pushy to the new girls in HR. They chose well normally; she had a crack team. *Damn it.* She realised that there was no option now. He'd forced her hand. She needed to speak to Harry after all. She couldn't let the dawn rise without at least a conversation. And what a conversation that was going to be.

Taking a moment to close the office door, she looked around first to see if she might be interrupted. She needed this to go well, with no distractions. Satisfied, she sat back down at her desk, took out her phone and looked for the number in her contacts. One she had called only once in the last few years, and never thought to be calling again. Not in her right mind, anyway.

Harry answered on the second ring, denying her any real opportunity to steel herself.

'Hello,' he said softly. She could hear the surprise in his voice. 'I'm so glad you called.'

'Hi,' she said shakily. 'It was you at the airport today then. I wasn't sure I hadn't had a small stroke and imagined the whole thing.'

He laughed, just once. 'Yeah, it was me. I'm sorry it happened that way. I wanted to speak to you properly, but I know it wasn't the best timing. How's Frank?'

She rolled her eyes, biting the skin on the inside of her mouth at her own stupid remark. To his credit, he didn't say anything else for a beat.

'It wasn't the best surprise,' she offered. 'He's fine. He got discharged.'

'That's good to hear. I didn't know you would be there though, truly. I was planning on telling you I was back in a better way.'

So he wasn't denying it then, or trying to play it down. He was telling the truth at least. Still, the job news was still ringing in her head. She needed to get control of this, get out in front of it. Before she clapped eyes on him again. There would be no running tomorrow. That was his forte, not hers. She wouldn't give him the satisfaction of seeing her squirm.

'Well, I would have guessed, given that you're due to start at the station tomorrow.'

Another pause.

He's wriggling like a worm on a hook.

She felt mean for thinking it, but she had feelings. Who knew? She was having all the feelings and being tired and exhausted after work wasn't helping. She needed to get this out. She needed to get off the phone, because even listening to his voice right now was too much. It was so much easier to pretend that she was over him when he wasn't around. Having him around was torture.

'It doesn't matter anyway. We worked together before. I suppose we can again.'

'I—' he started to cut in, but she couldn't let him. She'd lose the opportunity.

'Let me finish. When you left, I was in a

bit of a state. Nice job, by the way. Waiting till the airport to tell me. Just lovely, really.'

She heard Harry suck in a sharp breath, and she kept talking.

'Five weeks after, I found out I was pregnant. I'd been on a few nights out with Tom and Lloyd, some of the nurses. I told them I'd had a one-night stand and—'

'You slept with someone straight after I left?' His voice was louder now, a tinge of anger running through his words. 'Is that what you're telling me? You got pregnant?'

'Shut up, please! No, I haven't slept with… anyone since you.'

Damn it. Don't talk about that.

'Not that it's any business of yours what I did after you left, but the baby was yours, Harrison.'

'Mine?' he echoed, his voice softer now.

'Yes. Is yours, in fact. My son, Aidan. He's seven, he lives with me. People think he was the result of a one-night stand because I told them that's what happened, but he's yours.'

She sighed heavily, sitting back in her chair. She felt lighter, light-headed even. She'd spoken her truth. The only other person she'd told wasn't here to tell her story. Her mother had taken that secret well, but telling a headstone was different from a living person. They couldn't give an opinion, for one thing. She figured the people around her had their suspicions, but she'd always shut them down. It was too hard to even think about Harry, let alone have people pitying her for choosing to have the child of the man who'd left her in the dust. Or telling him that she was having his baby. He'd ignored her calls, every one of them, and she hadn't called to tell him the baby news. Why should she? He'd gone and blocked them all.

She didn't want to co-parent a child with someone who lived in another country. She'd never had a dad, and she didn't want Aidan to grow up with a part-time dad. She'd protected her son. You couldn't miss what you'd never had, she figured. Though it was getting harder now Aidan was getting older. The questions had already started with gusto, and it was just easier to continue with her story. That his dad was someone she didn't have any contact with, that they didn't need him in their lives.

At the other end of the phone there was a resounding silence. She could hear him breathe, so she carried on.

'I just needed you to know, since you will probably meet him at work, or someone will say something, or mention him, so…that's it. That's why I called. Just so you had the facts.'

'Why didn't you tell me?'

She closed her eyes, listening to the hurt in his voice.

'What was I supposed to do, Harry, call you up and tell you? You left, remember? I tried for weeks to get you to talk to me. I called your work. They said you were unavailable; they wouldn't even tell me anything about you. What was I supposed to do, ship him off every once in a while to Dubai to a man he didn't know? I didn't even know if you would want to be his father. For all I knew, you had a wife and kids out there. You chose to leave, and I didn't want him not to have his father. I've had that myself, and it's not a nice feeling. Better no father than one who doesn't show up for his kid. We've done okay this far on our own. If you'd called me back, just once, I would have told you. But you didn't, Harry, and I made peace with it.'

Another lie, she told herself. It was only her pride that had stopped her calling when Aidan was born, and Lord knows she had wanted to. Giving birth without him had felt so wrong. Every time Aidan had done something amazing she'd wanted to pick up the phone. When he took his first steps, said his first word. Dada. Oh, how she had cried at that. Her gorgeous, perfect little boy saying that word had broken her heart all over again. By then it had been too hard to call him. What could she say? Our secret son said his first word today?

'I'm sorry, I wasn't attacking you. It's just… a lot. I didn't expect this. We need to meet.'

Annabel was already shaking her head, before she remembered he couldn't see her. Thank goodness he couldn't, because she had silent tears rolling down her face and her hands were shaking.

'I don't think so,' she said finally. 'I don't want to see you, Harry. You had your chance.'

Harry was sitting outside his father's house, the hum of the hire car's engine ringing in his ears. He was a father. *A father.* To a boy already half grown, no less.

A dad was something he had never thought he would be. Or could be. When he'd found a lump on his testicle a few weeks before Dubai, he'd known that the signs were bad. He'd been so tired lately, his health not what it was. He knew it was more than the intensity of the job, the stress of the planned move, and this was it— testicular cancer. When he'd burned his life back home to the ground and headed out to Dubai, determined to kick the cancer before getting Annabel back, he'd woken up that first morning in his new life with another lump to obsess over.

His new bosses had been amazing. He'd called to tell them he couldn't take the job, what he was facing, and they'd not only protected his job, they'd told him to come anyway and be treated at their world class centre.

The second lump was more bad news, and it had taken the best expertise of the team he was supposed to be working with to keep him alive, and it had cost him his fertility.

The cancer was the reason he'd left Annabel behind. He'd seen what a toll her mother's cancer had taken on her and he couldn't bear the thought of her being his carer, all alone in a new country without her friends, nursing him with a cancer that the oncology department at the hospital in London didn't seem too optimistic about. He knew enough to know that the emergency scans they had done weren't good. He'd had a choice: stay home with a father who he didn't get on with, or go to his new life and fight to stay alive.

He'd been scared, but Annabel had been the deciding factor. He couldn't put her through that. He was Harrison Carter, strong, self-assured, always the first to run to a call. He didn't want Annabel to see him sick, or worse. She had been offered a job at the ambulance station where they'd trained. She was top of the class. She had a life to step into and he didn't want to ruin that for her. She'd wanted this her whole life and she was so close to getting it.

So he'd broken her heart, told her it wasn't working out, that he wanted to travel to Dubai on his own, and he'd left her there. Walking through the security gate, listening to her sob and call his name as he strode away from her. He didn't even look back, because he didn't want her to see his own tears.

As time had gone on and he'd found out he couldn't have children, going home had seemed an impossibility. What could he offer her, after all? What if the cancer came back, or she wanted children? He didn't want to derail her life all over again, so once more he'd chosen to protect her heart over his. Right then and there he knew he wouldn't go back to London. He couldn't get the all-clear and rock up at home with a ring. Not when it would only ever be the two of them. He knew that Annabel wanted children. They both did; they'd spoken of it often. An abstract vision for the future that they'd always assumed they would be able to fulfil when the time was right. Working abroad, saving up and seeing the world, then returning home to buy the house they'd always liked as kids and raising their little family.

Knowing that he would be returning home after so long with only the promise of the two of them together, he knew it wouldn't be fair. He'd broken her heart once and he didn't want to do it again. She could be happy with someone else, have the family she'd always wanted. He would just be a footnote in the story of her life. A bad, abandoning ex-boy-friend.

But now he knew that he should have come back all along. He should have flown home and fought harder. He was such a coward and look what it had cost them both. He'd ruined both their lives, and their son had been caught in the crossfire. Life was cruel but, thinking about Annabel's news, all he could feel was happiness right now. He had a child with the love of his life. That was something he'd never imagined post cancer. Hearing that he'd left her pregnant was just too cruel a twist of fate to comprehend right now. He felt as if the universe was laughing at him.

'I get why you don't want to meet, but I have so many questions,' he said eventually, his throat feeling dry. 'Does he know about me?'

Annabel winced, stuttering a little. 'No. I told him I'd just met his father the once. The same as I told everyone.'

Harry could feel the shock wash over him, his nerve-endings tingling. 'You didn't tell anyone the truth? I can't believe it.'

'No, and I don't need your judgement. You'd just left, you weren't talking to any of us. I made up a story. People were mad enough at you, and I couldn't bear their judgement. I get that you're mad but—'

'No. Well, yes, I am, but…thank you.'

'Thank you? What the hell for?'

He closed his eyes in frustration. 'I just mean…thank you. I know that sounds stupid but thank you. I don't deserve it, any of it. I'm so sorry I didn't call. I'm sorry I put you in that position.'

'I did it for me,' Annabel said coldly. 'And Aidan. I didn't want him to know about you, that you left us both without a backward glance. You coming back has forced my hand.'

'I know, but I don't want to hurt you or him. That's the last thing I want. Listen, can I meet him? I'd like to meet him. I'm just outside Dad's at the minute, but—'

Abe... He had another conversation or twenty coming then. 'Sorry, I didn't mean to push. I just— How is he? How did you manage...?' His voice trailed off. 'Are you with anyone?'

She huffed out a breath. 'Since I admitted I hadn't slept with anyone since you left me for dust, barefoot and pregnant, I guess I don't need to answer that. Meeting Aidan is another matter. I'll need to think on it. I have to think about him. He's gone through a lot recently.'

She sounded angry, guarded, and he couldn't blame her. He wanted to reply but he was too busy trying to get his size ten foot out of his mouth. He needed the next words to be clear, and to come out right.

'Annabel, I didn't mean it like that. I guess I'm just adjusting. I do have things to tell you though, a lot of things. Can we meet—just us, I mean? Without Aidan.' Just hearing him saying his name felt weird. 'Aidan.' He said it again. 'I like his name.'

'I don't think we should. Listen, you're working with me tomorrow; we'll have a lot to get through.' Harry heard a beep on the line, and Annabel spoke again. 'I have to go, I have another call. It's Aidan, I'm due to pick him up from his friend's house. I should go.'

'Wait…er…' He didn't know what he was going to say, but he had to get it out. 'You don't want me to see him, do you?'

Her hesitation made his heart stop. She didn't want him to meet her son. Their son. He'd really screwed everything up.

You're an idiot, Harry. What did you expect? The red carpet treatment? Two years of treatment and follow-ups, five years in remission, and almost a year to pack up his old life. All time away from his little family. All for nothing. He'd lost everything all over again. And more.

He held his breath, waiting for her next words.

'No,' she said eventually. 'I didn't tell you

about Aidan expecting anything. You came back, so you needed the facts. That's it. Nothing more. We have a life, Harry. One that doesn't involve you. I told myself I would tell you the truth if I ever saw you again.'

She paused for a minute, trying and failing to keep her voice steady. She couldn't let him in now; she just couldn't bear the risk. She wouldn't survive another Harry heartbreak. 'You are my past, Harry, and I want you to stay that way. I'll see you in the morning, ready to work.'

She could feel herself start to cry again, and she ended the call before he could respond. There, she'd done it. She'd been true to her son, and herself.

When Aidan had been born, Tom was her birth partner. Her friends had been there for the whole pregnancy. Abe had been the parent she needed. Her shock about the baby and disappointment at Harry had been tangible, and she'd kept her distance from the deeper conversations. They'd all just circled each other: Annabel broken-hearted, reeling from the news that she was expecting, Abe helping her where he could in practical terms. He'd even told the station that she was in a position to take the job. To their credit, they'd pulled together as a team through her maternity leave, and when she was ready the job was hers to step back into. As hard as that was, with a baby to raise and a career to keep on track.

She'd almost folded and told Abe the truth so many times. Aidan was his grandson after all. He had played the role since Aidan was a baby bump, but she'd never told him they were blood. With her friends and colleagues, it had been slightly easier. She hated pity and that would have been one big party. Annabel herself had never thought that way, not once she'd held Aidan in her arms in that hospital room. Tom had gone home to rest, and he and Lloyd were coming to collect her and the baby later that afternoon. She had the support, the friends, the family.

Abe had scooped her up that day at the airport and had been steadfastly on her side ever since. If he had been speaking to Harry, that would be a different matter. She wouldn't have put Abe in that position, but they'd fallen out before Aidan left for Dubai. Abe was stubborn in many ways, and he had never hidden the fact that he'd wanted Harry to become a GP, take the practice on after his retirement.

She didn't know if they'd ever spoken after those first few months of getting radio silence, and she knew never to ask. It wasn't fair on Abe to do so. That was down to Harry too. He'd walked away from them all without a backwards glance. He'd never even told his friends.

When she'd looked at the newborn child in her arms, the child who looked so much like her now, she'd promised him that he would never be left behind. She'd promised herself that day in the maternity ward that if Harry ever surfaced again she would tell him about his son, but that would be it. He wouldn't be given any opportunities to wreck the boy's life as he had theirs. Not a chance. She knew what having a wayward father did to a child, she'd experienced it first-hand, and the toll it had taken on her mother. Aidan knew that his dad wasn't around, that his mummy loved him very much. All true. Till now.

The questions would get harder as he grew, she knew, and they had, but that was the promise she'd made that day, and even though she'd questioned her decision many times over the years, she'd stuck to it. She wasn't the one who didn't know how to treat people, or to honour the promises she made. Aidan knew he had a father. He just didn't know him. He was an abstract part of his life, and Annabel wasn't about to confuse him by telling him the truth.

Harry was back to work tomorrow at the station and work they would. Hell, she'd been through worse times lately. Like the night she'd called Harry and begged him to come home, almost confessing her love for him still. He'd ruined that second chance too.

CHAPTER TWO

Six months earlier...

ANNABEL TOOK ANOTHER swig of her drink and gripped the phone tight. She was more than tiddly now, and she was grateful for the numb sensation it provided. She never would have got the courage to call otherwise. Her inhibitions were well and truly lowered.

'Sometimes I despise you for leaving me here alone, to face all of this. When I'm tired, or on days like today. I needed you today, more than I ever have since you left. I really needed you and guess what, you weren't there!'

She flicked her glass around her, gesturing wildly and splashing some of the contents down herself. Aidan had been given the all-clear after his fall in the school gym, and Tom was staying with him that night in the hospital to give her the night off before he came home. His head injury had been terrifying, but with the fear and worry, adrenalin had kicked in. Once Aidan was in the clear and was due home, all that had left Annabel and instead of relief she'd felt sad. And angry. Both aimed at Harry.

When Aidan had hit his head, it had crossed her mind that her son might die. She saw it all the time in her job. People took a little tumble and that was it. Lights out. Then she'd thought of Harry, miles away and utterly unaware that his son could have died. A son he didn't even know about. Instead of getting showered and going straight to bed, she'd opened a bottle of something strong instead, and the swirl of guilt had wrapped itself around her mind again. He should be here to see his son. She'd picked up the phone and dialled his number. She had a lot to say, even if it was into a voicemail void.

'Sometimes, you know, I have whole conversations with you in my head. I lie awake some nights, tearing a strip off you mentally. But what's the point, eh? You never hear me.

You won't even get this. You probably didn't get any of the messages we sent. I doubt you even kept your old number. I don't even know why I bothered. Nostalgia, probably. It's been a funny kind of week. An awful, scary week. If you do ever get this, Harry—' Sigh. 'Come home. Just come home. You've missed out on so much already. You'll never know just how much. It could have been so different, you know? I—' Even in her haze, she stopped herself short of telling him about Aidan. It wasn't something she wanted to tell him in a message over the phone. The thought of never knowing whether he'd heard it would be too much for her to take and obsess over.

'Just please…come home. I still lo— I want you to come home. I don't want some phone call to say you're sorry. It means nothing. Just…just get here. Be here for the people that need you, Harry.'

Clicking the off button with an unsteady hand, she pushed the phone away from her on the table. Even in her drunken state, she knew that she'd just dropped the ball. Or, more like, an epic clanger. She'd meant every word, but she'd never gone as far as actually telling him that. She had never let herself get that low, that weak before. She felt as if she'd just rolled over and showed him her soft underbelly. The same spot that she usually kept covered with her daily applied armour. She hated herself a little for it. Thank God she was too drunk to call him again and take it all back. She'd shown enough weakness for one day.

Sitting in her flat, she wondered to herself how things had got so bad. How the girl standing in that airport wouldn't recognise the life she now had. And she couldn't one hundred per cent attest to the fact that the old her would have done things differently. Now, after almost losing her son to a stupid slip at school, she couldn't seem to be anything but mad. Mad that she was doing everything on her own. Dealing with the guilt she felt over her decision to keep the two people she cared about the most apart. Not all times were bad, after all. Many, if not most, of her happy memories pre-Aidan involved Harry, and Tom and some of the others on the team that had stuck around after qualifying.

She tortured herself wondering what Harry had been doing all this time. Was he even still in Dubai? For all she knew, he was married now. Had his own family to look after. How would Aidan fit into that? She didn't want another mother helping to raise her child. It was another one of the reasons she'd never told him. The more time that passed, the harder it might be.

Harry heard Annabel end the call, the line clicking off in his ear as he stood in the night. His father's house was right in front of him, his old estate car still sitting in the drive. Everything looked the same, if a little smaller. It felt smaller to him, but at this moment in time he didn't trust his eyes. He was still reeling from the bombshell that Annabel had dropped on him.

I have a baby son. No, he was nearly eight years old now. Hardly a baby. There'd been no sign that Annabel was pregnant before he'd left for Dubai. He knew she was telling the truth, but it didn't help him any. Now, instead of just feeling the shame and regret of walking out on his life, he also had to reconcile the fact that he'd missed out on meeting his son. Of course Annabel didn't want him to meet him. Why would she? He'd done nothing in the last near decade that would give her any reason or inclination to do so.

He'd walked away to protect Annabel, and that had meant cutting everyone else off too. It had been the only way. And now he was cowering outside his father's house, wondering what the hell he was going to walk into this time. What would his father say about this? He'd obviously kept his own call from Annabel too. Whether that was to protect her or his wayward son, he had no idea. He guessed he was about to find out.

Six months ago, he'd picked up the drunken message from Annabel. He'd been on shift, and when he checked his pocket and saw the missed call he could have wept. From fear or happiness, he didn't know. Then panic had set in. She'd stopped calling years ago—why call now? When he saw she'd left a voicemail he'd rung his father straight away, not wanting to listen to the news that she must have been calling about. Bad news from home. That must have been why she'd called. Given the fact that they'd both grown up for the most part with one parent and no other family other than the one they'd made for themselves, it was easy to make the connection. She was obviously just passing on some unavoidable item of news. Why else would she be calling, right?

When his dad had answered he'd felt more than relief. He'd also felt a sudden longing deep within him, a feeling that if he could have clicked his fingers to be transported back home, he would have. When his surprised dad had rung off, seemingly believing his son when he'd said he just wanted to say hello, that he'd been thinking about him, the feeling hadn't left him. He was healthy now. He was cancer free, all signed off. He'd built a life in Dubai. He had friends, even been on the odd date or two. It was a life but, hearing from the two ghosts from his past that still seemed to haunt him, he realised that he was done in Dubai. Infertility be damned. He wanted out. When he played the voicemail from Annabel, basically berating him for not being there, begging him to come home, he knew what he had to do. He'd called his dad back.

'Hello?'

'Hi, Dad. It's me again. Listen, I lied just now. Annabel called me.'

He heard the television being turned down in the background, and his father spoke again.

'Well, I didn't think you just rang to say hello after all this time of ignoring us. What did she say?'

'She told me off, basically.'

Abe chuckled. 'Sounds about right. What else?' he pressed.

'Nothing. She told me to come home. She said I should be there for the people I left behind.'

'She's got a point, son. Took you a while. Did she sound okay?'

'I think she might have been a little drunk, sad maybe. Everything okay back home?'

Abe sighed, a deep sigh that filled the silence between them. 'She's had better times, but it's not for me to say. What are you going to do? It's obviously rattled you. Are you okay?'

'Yeah, I'm okay. I stayed in Dubai. I don't know what to say. Is anything I say going to make up for what I did?'

'With me? Ah, son, I'm just glad to hear you're alive. You're not asking about me, though. What are you going to do about Annabel?'

'I'm going to listen to her, Dad. I'm going to get the next flight back.'

'No son, that's not a good idea. Not now. Not on impulse.'

'What do you mean, not now?'

Another sigh. His dad was being cagey, and about a thousand scenarios ran through Harry's mind.

'Is she getting married or something, is that what this is? Is she sick?' The big C word swam round his head. It had taken enough from their lives, but cancer didn't care how many times it took a bite out of a family.

'No, son, no. Nothing like that. Listen, you

just dropping in for a flying visit is going to do more harm than good, believe me. I think you know that, if you're honest with yourself. Have you thought this through? She rang you for weeks, Harry, after you left her like that. You put that girl through hell. One call from her now and you're ready to come back. What's happened?'

Harry bit the corner of his lip. 'Nothing, Dad. Listen, back then…it was complicated. I was a different person. A stupid, scared and immature person. Don't you want me to come home?'

'I never wanted you to leave in the first place.' There was a snap in his tone.

'I know, Dad, I know that. Listen, can we not fight?'

Abe sighed. 'I don't want to fight, son. I regret that fight so much. I feel like I pushed you to go to Dubai, to get away from your old man.' He sighed heavily. 'I know I pushed you too hard, but it was only ever meant with love. Son, I want the best for you. And Annabel. You're still working, right? I assume you have a contract?'

Harry gripped the phone tight, looking around the locker room he was standing in. 'Yeah, I have a few months left on this one.'

'Well, then. You have obligations. You can't just up and leave. It's not the best time. Let things calm down a while, okay?'

'Dad, are you sure about this? Do I call her or what? Are you sure she's okay?'

'Yes, son, and I wouldn't call her. It's not the right time. Your first meeting can't be on the phone. There's too much to say. Trust me, I want to help you, but listen to me. Stay where you are. Let's talk again soon, okay?'

Harry sighed, the adrenalin from the call leaving him. 'Okay, Dad. Listen, I'd better go. I'm not finished on shift yet, and my break's nearly over.'

'Okay, son, you take care. Remember what I said. And Harry?'

'Yeah, Dad?'

'It's really nice to hear your voice, son. Don't leave it so long next time.'

Harry promised to call again soon, feeling homesick and torn in half with his emotions. This was why he'd never called before.

Ignoring people's existence didn't make you want to hop on a flight home. Hearing his father's voice, and Annabel's, all in one night had torn down the defences he'd built up all these years. Denial and hiding were wonderful things, but it only took a small chink in the armour to show the cracks.

He'd stayed away for so many reasons, but he realised now he just had to take his shot. He had to go home, to put the past to bed if nothing else. He didn't want to be an old man full of regrets. He'd done the deathbed revelations. When the treatment had made him weak and scared, all he'd wanted was his family around him. He didn't want to be there again, years from now, with nothing but empty chairs around him.

The next day he gave notice on his job and made plans to come back to London. It was time. Annabel wanted him to come home, and he wanted to be there. He didn't tell his dad. With his notice period, he figured enough dust would have settled. He couldn't wait any more. He'd wasted enough time already. He had to take his shot, try to get the life he wanted back. He just didn't know at the time what that would look like. Certainly not discovering that he was a father—something he'd long given up on. He had to face his father too, which was an ordeal in itself. He felt weighed down more than usual with the guilt of disappointing the people he loved the most.

He was still standing on his father's front path when he saw the curtains start to twitch in the neighbouring properties. Abe still lived in the house connected to his GP practice and he ran the place like a small village surgery, not like one of the many larger health centres in the big smoke. He was all about the people, and the care he could give to them. He lived and breathed their little community and had meant to keep it in the family. With a reluctant and unwilling son, that was never going to happen. They had had an uneasy relationship for years before Harry left. Made even more awkward by him leaving as he had.

They'd not spoken since the call home, but he had emailed his dad a couple of times. Just to say hello, nothing about coming home. He didn't want Abe to talk him out of it or tell Annabel. He had wanted to come home and see her for himself, but that had gone out of the window the second Frank Jessop had hit the deck.

Swallowing hard and trying not to look too suspicious to the neighbours, he started to walk up the path towards the main house. He was just about to knock when the door opened, and there was Abe. The two men eyed each other for a long moment and then Harry saw the handset in his father's hand. Lifting the receiver to his ear, he smiled for the person on the phone as he spoke, but the look he fixed his son with didn't convey any joy.

'I'd better let you go, love. No, no….' he placated the person on the phone, moving aside to allow his son to enter the house. The lamp in the hallway lit his way and Harry walked in, letting his father finish his conversation while he looked around the place. Abe didn't exactly keep office hours; some of his patients rang him to discuss soap operas, or to ask about their latest health niggle.

Abe's door was always open. Ever the medical professional. Like father, like son in that respect, if not much else.

The house looked much the same. The decor had been changed, sure, but Abe's knick-knacks were all still there. The stack of books on his side table, science fiction and medical journals, mostly. The TV was on in the corner, a soap opera paused on the screen; the mug of tea on the coffee table was still steaming. It seemed Abe had already been interrupted from his quiet evening.

He could hear his father speaking in hushed tones in the kitchen, but Harry didn't try to listen. His attention had been distracted anyway, by a collection of photos that he hadn't seen before, all framed and in pride of place on the mantelpiece above the old coal fire. Another thing Abe was known for. His reluctance for change outside the world of medicine was legendary. The man would lick a yoghurt pot clean rather than waste a drop, and he hated technology in the home. He also wasn't one for photos, but his collection had grown by the looks of things.

Harry smiled to himself as he looked closer at the photo of the three of them on Brighton beach, years back when he was a young kid who'd dreamed of being a superhero in medical clothing. Abe, his mother and he were all huddled together, wrapped in a towel and wet from their dip in the sea. It was one of his favourite memories of his mother, of them together. Abe had been different back then too. Funnier, more at ease.

Perhaps Mum was the one that held us together too. Without her, we were both a bit lost.

He could hear Abe ending his call, talking about meeting up the next day.

Still just as committed.

Harry smiled to himself. Some things never changed. He went to put the photograph back on the mantelpiece and his gaze fell to the one sitting next to it. It was of Abe, holding a fishing rod and seemingly laughing his head off on the pier. A young boy was waggling a crab at him, no fear showing on his cute little face. It wasn't an old photo, and the boy wasn't him. They had done that over the years, but he didn't recognise the boy. He looked familiar somehow.

A voice behind him almost made him drop the frame. 'So, you came home then.'

Abe was standing in the doorway now, in his uniform of shirt and tie, the phone still in his hand. His expression was closed off, and he looked tired.

'Yeah, I did. I thought I'd come say hello.' He gave himself a moment. 'I'm starting at the old station in the morning. Permanently.'

To his credit, Abe didn't react. He didn't drop the phone or ask fifty-five questions about what Harry had been doing for the best part of the last decade. Or why in the last six months he hadn't bothered to mention that he was returning home. In fact, he didn't say much at all. He just stood there, staring at Harry as though he were a mirage.

'Nothing to say?' Harry tried, feeling the familiar sting of rejection. He wasn't a child any more, but it hurt that his relationship with his father was so stilted. With a pang, he re-alised that he had repeated the pattern, albeit unknowingly. His son was seven years old and he didn't even know his father.

Harry felt his head drop, the long flight and the events of the day catching up with him. His dad walked right up to him and pulled him into a hug. Harry was shocked for a moment, but wrapped his arms around him and hugged him tight. Abe was clinging onto him tightly, patting his back as the two men held each other. Pulling away, his dad smiled at him.

'I'm glad you're back, son. I really am.' He pulled him back in for another hug, and Harry felt the sting of tears.

'Me too, Dad.' Eventually, Abe released him, walking past him into the lounge. Instead of sitting back in his chair, he walked up to the liquor cabinet, putting the phone down and reaching for his best whisky. Harry didn't move till his father was holding out a full crystal glass tumbler in his direction. They both sat down, Abe in his chair and Harry on the couch. As he sat back, he felt something stab him. Something sharp. Reaching behind him, he pulled out a plastic dinosaur. He laughed, putting it on the arm of the sofa.

'Patients still coming in for a cuppa, eh? Someone's missing a Velociraptor.'

Abe sat back in his chair, taking a deep sip of his drink before eyeing his son again. He nodded to the photo Harry had just been looking at.

'It belongs to that little boy. He's mad on dinosaurs.' Another moment of awkward silence. 'So, you're staying for good? No fancy job to go back to?'

Harry felt like laughing as he considered his father's words. If only he knew how fancy it hadn't been at times. How he'd helped save lives in the sticky heat, after battling for his own life. It wasn't all sand and opulence. He'd worked hard, saved up, kept a low profile. He'd stuck to the plan, to create a career. Spent many nights in his bed, thinking of the woman he'd left behind. Wishing she was there, sleeping beside him. Smiling at him over the breakfast table. Dragging him to see the sights on their days off. She'd been a ghost in Dubai, always following him wherever he went.

No other woman compared to her. In his mind, he'd never completely left her. He'd just walked away from everything else. With the job and his cancer, it had been all he could take. All he could focus on. He hadn't wanted Annabel to deal with all that. He didn't want her to derail her life and end up as a nursemaid to him. Looking back, he realised that he hadn't been expecting to survive it. The thought of dying and leaving her out there all alone had seemed much worse than leaving her behind back then. Now it seemed, had he taken her with him, they would have been going through it with a pregnancy to worry about too.

He looked at the dinosaur on the edge of the couch, picking it up and running his thumbnail along its back.

'Nope, I'm back for good.'

'You got a place to live yet?' Ever the pushy father.

'No, Dad, not yet. I'm booked into one of the airport hotels till I find somewhere. It's been a bit of a day.' He turned the little brown figure around in his hand.

I wonder what Aidan likes to play with. I don't know a thing about him. Will I ever?

Saying it had been a bit of a day was downplaying things, just a bit.

'I bet it has. Too busy to call home first, give us a heads-up?'

Us? Who was that on the phone? Are the jungle drums already banging away?

'You don't need a hotel.' Abe motioned in the direction of the staircase with the glass in his hand. The ice tinkled against the tumbler. 'Your room's right there. Cancel the reservation, stay here.' He cleared his throat. 'You should be close for work, you know. It's fine, I have the room.'

He was trying to play it down now, but Harry was really touched by the sentiment. He kept fiddling with the dinosaur, his dad now pressing play on the television and settling back down in his chair. After the show had ended and they still hadn't said anything, Harry decided to talk.

'I came back because of Annabel's call,

Dad. She told me I'd ducked out of life for long enough, and she was right. I know you said it wasn't good to come back then, but I waited. I worked my notice; I gave up my place. I'm back. I even got my old job back.'

Abe side-eyed him, his eyes narrowing to slits when he saw the little plastic toy in Harry's hand. 'Is that all you came back for? Don't go breaking that either. It belongs to Aidan.'

Harry's eyes snapped to his. His fist clenched around the dinosaur toy. 'What did you just say?'

Abe sighed and, shaking his head at his son, he dropped his head. 'Cut the crap, son. The dinosaur is Aidan's. The boy in the photo is Annabel's son. He calls me Granddad. Catch up.' Before Harry could even try to retort, Abe had turned the television up again.

Harry looked at him, aghast. Looking from his father to the mantelpiece, he studied the photo. It was Annabel staring back at him. He could see it now. The little boy had her hair, her look. He stood and picked up the photo, looking at the others and seeing Aidan there too. The photos were all of Aidan. Aidan and his mum. Aidan and Abe. Aidan in his first school uniform.

He recognised Annabel's flat in the background, the one she had once shared with her mother. It was all here, his life laid out. Somehow, Annabel had raised this child without him, without even telling anyone the truth. He felt a stirring of anger, but he knew deep down it was misplaced. How could he be mad at her after everything? He knew Annabel well enough to know that she would have made Aidan her priority. He couldn't hate her for that. He loved her for it.

He wanted to shout at his dad though, for not calling him. He'd known all along, judging from the photographs. The similarities were obvious. Why hadn't he picked up the phone? He had so many questions, but one shouted loudest in his head. Turning to his dad, he clenched his jaw.

'Why didn't you tell me?'

Abe jumped at his words, and the television was swiftly turned off. Turning to look at him, his face determined now, he walked over to his son and embraced him in another hug. Harry being so much bigger than he, Abe chose to wrap his arms around Harry's waist. He squeezed him tight.

'Annabel never told me, but I knew. I'm not stupid, I did the math. We weren't exactly on speaking terms, were we? She told everyone a story, and she had no one in her corner. I love that boy; Aidan is the best thing you ever did. It made losing you that bit more bearable, if I'm honest. I missed you, son. I regret so much of our time together. I'm so sorry I was so pushy. I should have been a better father, but being a grandfather is the best thing ever. I was there for him, and he knows about you. I've told him so many stories about you over the years. I wanted to tell you, but it wasn't my decision. Can you forgive me?'

Harry looked at his dad, and nodded slowly. 'I get it, Dad. I don't like it, but I get it. How can I make any of this right?'

'You ask that very question, son, you ask that very question.' Patting him on the back like he used to when he was a boy, Abe gripped his hand tight. 'Welcome home, son. We have some work to do.'

Annabel Sanders was a shadow of her former self the next morning as she walked into work. She'd barely got a wink of sleep, moving from side to side in the king-size bed she'd splurged on as a housewarming present to herself. Aidan's room was finished, the first room she'd tackled as soon as she'd got the keys to her dream house. It wasn't a shiny new-build on some labyrinth estate, but very much a fixer-upper. Maud, the old lady who'd lived there for many years, had passed the year before and with the life insurance her mother had left her and almost all her savings it was just about enough. She'd bought Elm House, the very house she'd walked and driven past growing up. The one she and Harry had once dreamed of buying together. That would be another awkward conversation.

I hope he doesn't read anything into it. We are definitely done. We were done the minute he boarded that plane. So what if he still makes my stomach flip? That's just chemistry. It will fizzle out.

She headed into Reception, using her key card to buzz through to the main ambulance station. As soon as she walked in she was switched on, all business. She ran the handover, the meeting room full of incoming staff, ready to work. It had been a quiet night all in all, but there had been reports of some gang-related tensions in the area. Often this meant injuries, RTAs. They liaised with the police regularly and kept their eyes and ears open.

She was just addressing the team on the issue when the door at the back of the room opened and in slid Harry. A couple of people looked to the door to see who had entered, and a few more did a double-take. One of the nurses, Purdie, was one of them and the glance she flashed Annabel almost made her garble her words. She kept it short and professional, eager to both get on with the calls and get out of the spotlight. She looked at Harry, and he was watching her. He had a small smile on his face and when their eyes locked she felt her mouth go dry. It felt as if her tongue had doubled in size. She took a breath and dismissed her team.

'Let's get out there, guys. Stay vigilant, and let's have a good day.' People were just starting to leave when she spoke again. 'Carter.' She addressed him by his surname, as their colleagues often did in work hours, as a quick shorthand, looking at him and acknowledging him. 'You're with me. Ambulance seventeen.' She figured it was better to get off on the right foot. Show the people she worked with that Harry was just another staff member to her and she was still in control. Try to cut the gossip short before it engulfed her whole.

Harry pushed away from his leaning position against the wall, and it was then she noticed that he was in full uniform. She'd not even noticed it when he'd walked in; all she had focused on was his face. She swallowed down the wave of nostalgia as she kept her eyes on his. She couldn't read him, and it irritated her. Even after all the years that had separated them, she'd always thought that she would be able to read him.

What is he thinking, after our conversation? Is he going to let it drop?

'No problem, Sanders.' He said it easily, fitting back into his old role as easily as she did hers for the onlookers around them, even though their locked eyes said differently to each other. The room was full, thick with murmurs. Neither of them heard any of them. They just stared at each other.

Is he trying to read me too?

She returned his curt nod, and then the moment was broken. He was gone.

What is it about that man? I can't help but watch him leave. And wish he would come back.

People were on the move and he was swallowed by uniforms and the swish-swish of the doors. Annabel was still looking when they swished closed for the final time. With a sigh, she started to head out when she noticed Purdie was still in her seat. Purdie was the bones of this place, even more than Annabel was. She was one of the best, and she never missed a blessed trick. She'd run the admissions ward when she'd first started there and then the cancer ward floor, and her nurses all adored her. She covered A&E on her days off, attending the briefings when she was on her overtime shifts. They ran like a tight, happy little ship. If Purdie had been a mama bear, they would all have been her cubs. Whether they liked it or not.

Annabel kept an eye on the door, trying to stride purposefully across the room on jelly legs, but Purdie stopped her as soon as she was in reach.

'Did you know he was coming?' she asked, straight to the point as ever.

'Did my shocked expression give me away?'

Purdie raised her dark eyebrows, reaching for Annabel's hand and pulling her down in the seat next to her.

'Thanks,' Annabel replied, her voice dull and flat. 'I think I'm about to keel over.'

'He's working here now, with you?'

Annabel could barely bring herself to nod. Her face felt numb, as if she couldn't control her expression any more.

'Well, I'll be… Takes a lot to shock me, but…' Purdie slapped her free hand on her thigh and covered her friend's hand with hers. 'Take a minute, catch your breath.'

The two women sat in silence, staring into space as they processed the news together.

'He looks good though, right? That tan, that hair?' She laughed a little, and Annabel snorted. 'Oh, come on, even you can admit he looks well. It's good to see. He's been in Dubai this whole time?'

Another numb-faced nod. 'I think so. Who knows?'

Purdie nodded. 'He's here alone?' Her voice was delicate now, measured.

'I don't know that either.' She hadn't even thought about it, but the phone call came screaming back to her. 'Yes, actually, I think he is.'

He came to talk to me, and I blindsided him with the news about Aidan. He didn't exactly give the impression that he had a wife and kids in tow. That's something to be grateful for. Because of how complicated things are, she lied to herself. *Not that I care either way.*

'Not about the work then, eh? Well, that changes things.'

Annabel frowned. 'How?'

Purdie put her arm around Annabel's shoulder and drew her in. Annabel went willingly, resting her head on her friend's shoulder. She smelled like Purdie always did. Comforting. Motherly.

'Believe me, my girl, that boy is back with a purpose in that head of his. If he's here alone, he's come to find something, not leave it behind.'

'He came for a job. Tom's job.'

Purdie laughed louder this time, her whole body jiggling with mirth and making Annabel's frazzled head bounce on her shoulder.

'If you think that man came all this way just to work here, looking at you the way he just did, then I have a feeling that we'll be having lots more conversations like these.'

Annabel groaned, burying her head further into the nurse's shoulder, and Purdie's deep, rich laughter filled the empty room once more.

'Great, I can't wait,' she said sarcastically, and Purdie laughed again.

'Things happen for a reason, child. I keep telling you that. You'll see.'

Annabel had a feeling that whatever was going to happen, she wouldn't really have a chance to avoid it anyway. What a pair they were, both ostriches with their heads in the hot Dubai sand. She needed a minute before she started her awkward day, cramped up in the ambulance with her old childhood sweetheart, the air thick between them like London smog.

'I guess I will,' she muttered, burying deeper into her friend's embrace.

Sitting in the front of the ambulance with Harry felt like stepping into a time machine. She could smell his aftershave as she buckled herself in, and it took all her concentration to focus on putting on her seatbelt without giving away how much she was dreading their first shift back together. Her two worlds were starting to collide, and not only had she not seen it coming, she'd even pushed them together herself.

Telling Harry about Aidan was something

she had tortured herself over for the longest time. Every time she saw Abe with Aidan, it was on the tip of her tongue to blurt out that Granddad wasn't just an honorary title, especially after all the support Abe had shown her since Harry left. It was a blood connection too. If Aidan had looked like a mini Harry the decision would have been made for her, but with him taking after her in the looks department she'd continued to lie. For a while there, she'd almost believed her own version of events. A one-night stand with a man who had vaporised into thin air. It was half true, so she'd made peace with it. Now Harry was back, and she had a feeling he was about to open a can of worms.

Her own feelings aside, she needed Aidan to be okay through all this. She needed to protect her son. That was the driving force behind the lie in the first place. After the time off school recovering from his injury, and the house move, the last thing the poor lad deserved was to get to know a person who wouldn't be around in a few months. She didn't know why Harry had come back, and that was keeping her up at night too. It had been six months since that disastrous phone call. He'd hardly thrown some clothes into a case and raced to the airport after her call, had he? She'd tossed and turned, thinking about the awkward day that lay ahead, and spent hours staring at the ceiling, worrying if she'd done the right thing by coming clean.

Aidan had been his usual full-of-beans self this morning, and she'd caught herself comparing him with the new Harry. The tanned stranger who had turned her life upside down for the second time. She'd never told anyone the truth about Aidan's parentage. She'd ridden out the stares and the whispered comments from those around her, judging her for sleeping with some stranger so soon after Harry had left. The obvious suspicions of those who knew her best. As her belly grew, more and more people asked questions, and she'd answered them all with a smile on her face. She knew the truth, and because people already blamed Harry for walking out she hadn't wanted the pity or stupid comments around her son.

She guessed, deep down, she hadn't wanted them to hate Harry any more either. Being in love with the man who'd left you pregnant and broken-hearted frankly sucked. She'd pitied herself enough; she didn't need any more from the people around her.

She didn't want to be that person ever again, feeling lost and out of control. It was directly at odds with her work persona. Over the years, the story had never changed from her lips, and gradually the questions stopped. Everyone at the station loved Aidan, and she was happy.

Am I? Today, I'm just not sure. I need sleep. That's it. It's the shock and the night of tossing the pillows on and off my bed.

She'd thought that Abe suspected something, back in those first few weeks when she did nothing but cry on his couch, her hormones making her heartbreak feel that much worse. He had never once asked about the father or told her that Aidan needed a father. He was the one person who had never shown anything but excitement and love for Aidan, and those things grew once Aidan was born.

He had been a grandfather to Aidan from day one, and with him and her friends she'd muddled through those first sleep-deprived months, and had childcare backup when she went back to work. Once her friend Teri was on board, having just had her own son Finn, she had a little army of willing carers to enable her to navigate those first few years.

Annabel tried to shake off her strange mood, looking across at Harry. He was strapped in, his body turned away from her as he looked out of the window. He looked relaxed, his back against the seat, his hands in his lap. To anyone else, he would have looked positively serene, but Annabel still knew his tells. The hands on his lap weren't still; he was tapping his fingers together, an old sign that he was feeling the tension.

Good, she thought, her old resentment waking her up. *You should suffer, Harry.*

Abe had an old saying; he'd told her it often over the years. *What doesn't kill you builds character.* Well, she'd had enough character-building for one lifetime. She was happy, she'd made peace with the past, as much as you could when you got ghosted by the love of your life. She *was* happy, till the minute she'd set eyes on him. Now, everything seemed skewed, off-kilter. As if he'd come back from the dead and no one had batted an eyelid.

Even Tom had been quiet on the subject since. Although preparing to be new parents meant he and Lloyd were really busy. Her problems weren't theirs, after all. Life went on. With her job, she knew how fragile life could be, how short and cruel sometimes too. She wished her mother were here to talk to. To talk about Harry coming back. She swallowed down the pain she felt and turned her mind back to the job.

'Ready to green up?' she asked, her finger on the button that told the station they were ready to take calls. 'We have Hillingdon today but, given the nightshift, we might have to switch things around.'

Harry turned away from the window. His hands stilled in his lap. 'I'm good to go. It might take me a minute to get acclimatised again, but I'm good.'

'Anything you're rusty on, just shout. I'll be the lead today anyway.'

He pointed out of the window at the road beyond the car park. 'Oh, it's not the medicine, more the location. It might take me a second to navigate around the old place.'

Old place. Wow, that was like a bullet to the heart. Arrogant too. Not the old Harry.

'Well, luckily, I still know the streets like the back of my hand.' She pressed the button, pulling out of the station because she just couldn't stand sitting there any longer. 'And I don't need a co-pilot.'

'Ambulance seventeen, request for help, Hillingdon, on the estate.'

Annabel looked up to the sky when the address was read out. It was on the next street from her old flat, and she felt as if her dear old mum was messing with her from above. Their first meeting had been at the airport, and now this.

The patient was Phyllis, a new ambulance service regular. She was in early dementia;

home care nurses came twice a day and her husband Jerry was well able to care for her. They only called for help when she fell, which was becoming more and more frequent as her condition worsened. Jerry couldn't lift her on his own, and falls in the elderly could be much more serious than they first looked. Picking up the radio handset, she radioed back that they were en route and flicked on the sirens and lights.

As they were heading towards the estate Annabel's new house loomed into view and she felt as if her heart might stop. The sold sign was still up out front, with no signs of life in the windows. The skip she'd hired for the building rubbish was sitting outside, half full. She saw Harry's head whip back to look as they sped past.

'The old house finally sold on, eh? Maud passed away? That's sad. Bless her.'

'Huh?' She turned the next corner, nodding to a driver who gave way to let them through. 'What house?' She felt as if her ears were on fire with the effort of acting dumb. Her whole face felt flushed. Catching sight of herself in the side mirror as she checked the traffic, all she saw were her own panicked eyes staring back at her.

'*The* house. From when we were kids—don't you remember?'

'Oh. Yeah, I remember. It might be better to concentrate on the job though.'

'Gotcha. All business.' He reached for the radio, telling the control desk that they had arrived at the address. As soon as she stopped the ambulance he was off into the back, pulling his kit on and grabbing the backboard. He didn't even acknowledge her, just headed to the door to the flats.

A worried-looking Jerry led the duo into the hallway of the flat, where Phyllis was now sitting up, smiling at Annabel.

'Hello!' she said jovially, giving them all a little wave. 'I can't get up.'

Jerry stepped to the side but stayed close by.

'I know, love. These are the paramedics, remember? They've come to help, and you remember Annabel.' Once upon a time, before she became ill, Phyllis had run the local nursery which Aidan had attended. She always seemed to remember her, even now. It helped, and when the calls came in they were usually given to Annabel if possible. It was easy to scare an already confused person just by being a stranger, especially one in uniform carrying scary-looking equipment.

'Annabel, how's the little fella doing?'

Annabel was standing right next to Harry, their shoulders brushed up against each other in the narrow space. She felt his body go rigid against her. As her brain scrambled for the right thing to say, she found herself wanting to tell him something about Aidan.

'He's great, Phyllis. He's loving his new bedroom and doing well at school. He says hello and sends his love.'

Phyllis beamed. 'He'll go far, that lad, I said, didn't I, Jerry? Footie still going well too?' Annabel was astonished at how good her memory was today. From Jerry's face, she could tell she wasn't the only one.

'Yeah, he's playing for the Hillingdon Wolves now, Under Eights.'

The same team his dad played for when

they were kids. Harry had the chance to turn professional, but he'd chosen medicine.

'Is that true?' Harry whispered beside her, his nose tickling her ear accidentally as he leaned in. She couldn't suppress the shudder that he evoked, but she recovered herself quickly.

Work, Annabel, work.

'Yes,' she whispered back to him. 'I don't lie.'

She moved closer to her patient, offering her hand.

'Come on then, Phyllis, let's get you sorted and off that floor.'

It was almost lunchtime when they finished their latest job and clocked off to eat. A woman had cut herself in her kitchen. A slip of the knife and she was now in the hospital getting stitched up for a minor cut. The poor woman was more upset about messing up her planned wedding anniversary dinner. Her husband couldn't have cared less about the dinner; he had just arrived in A&E, suit crumpled, tie askew. He'd searched for her the second he'd walked through the doors and, seeing her, his face had relaxed and he'd dashed over, cursing the traffic that had kept him from her side and scooping her into his arms.

She and Harry had watched them for a little while, and then departed silently. Annabel had driven to the sandwich shop near the community centre, and they were now sitting in the car park, hot coffees in their hands, food in paper bags on their laps.

'Annie, can we talk?'

She swallowed down her coffee rather gracefully, considering he'd spoken just as she was taking a mouthful of Americano.

'It's Annabel these days, and yes, we can talk.'

'When I left, I—'

Annabel felt the blood leave her face. She couldn't talk about that, not yet. She didn't want to feel the sting of rejection again. Not till she had recovered from his return at least.

'No, not about that. I thought you meant about Aidan, or the job.' She risked looking at him now, and he was looking back at her.

He looked wounded, and she hated herself for it.

'It's relevant to Aidan.' His jaw flexed and he took a long time to take his next drink of coffee. 'Why did you tell me about him if you don't want to talk about anything?'

'I didn't say I wanted to talk about the past, that's all. Can I not have a bit of time? I told you about Aidan because I always told myself if I saw you again, if you ever came back to London, I would tell you about him. You told me not to contact you, remember? You ignored me for weeks. You asked me to let you go. So I let go.' She bit her lip, mad at herself for breaking her own ruddy rule.

'You did contact me again though. Six months ago. You called me and told me to come home.' Annabel's sharp intake of breath caused his brow to furrow. 'I handed in my notice, but it took time.' He paused, as if to add something else, but shook his head as though dislodging the words from his throat. 'I was on a lengthy contract by then. I came home as soon as I could, Annie. I want to talk, about all of this. I'm staying with Dad now. I'm not far away.'

The last remark sent Annabel's eyebrows up to her hairline. 'Abe's letting you stay? Wow.'

Harry chuckled, but it died in his throat. 'Yeah, I was a bit surprised too.'

'He does know then.' She spoke her thoughts out loud, not able to stop them. 'About Aidan. He would have been straight on the phone if it was news to him.'

Harry nodded slowly. 'Yeah, he knows. I didn't tell him though. We spent half the night and his liquor cabinet last night talking about it.'

Annabel tried to speak but she felt as if someone had sat on her chest. 'Oh, what a mess,' was all she could croak out.

'You okay?'

He placed his hand on her arm but as soon as his fingertips touched her clothing, she pulled away infinitesimally.

'Is he…is he mad?' she choked out. 'I didn't want to keep it from him, but it was just easier at the time. I always thought that he just kind of knew. He's dealt with enough pregnant women to work out a due date.'

'No, of course he isn't. He loves being a granddad. He told me loads of stories about Aidan, when he was little. He could never be mad at you for giving him a grandchild. You should call him; he's not mad at all. He's pretty pleased, to be honest.'

'He's the best granddad,' she said, smiling now at the thought. 'Aidan adores him.'

Harry's face softened and he reached for her hand this time. She moved it away, taking out a sandwich to cover her snub. Harry clenched his fist for a second, and then reached for his own lunch.

'He knows why you did it. I understand too, though I don't like it. I also hate the thought that you were with someone else, even if he was imaginary. Was there really never a guy?'

The look of relief on his face when she shook her head made her stomach flip.

Don't start this game, missy. There's too much at stake to let him play with your emotions. You can bet the farm that he didn't spend his nights in bed, pining alone for the other half of himself.

'I won't ask the same about you,' she countered.

Another flex of the jaw from him.

'I had other things on my mind for a long time,' was all he gave her. 'And then I was busy with work. I went on a couple of dates, but it never came to anything. I wasn't looking. When I got your call, all I could think about was finishing my contract and getting back here. I just didn't expect this. I do want to see him though. I've seen photos of him at Dad's. He looks just like you.'

Annabel smiled, as she always did when someone mentioned her boy.

'Yeah, he does. He's got your stubborn streak though.' She laughed despite herself. It was so hard to be angry at him all the time. Just being around him made her head spin from annoyed to elated that this moment had come. She'd thought of telling him about Aidan so many times over the years, played the scenes out in her head. Not all of them were filled with recriminations and anger.

Some ended with them running off into the sunset together.

He came back because I asked him to. The day our son was nearly lost.

'Aidan had an accident at school. He fell off some gym equipment. It was pretty bad for a few days; he had a head injury, swelling on the brain. The day I called you, it was the day I found out he was going to be okay.'

His face fell, and this time his hand wrapped around hers with hesitation. She let him be.

'He's okay now though?'

Annabel nodded, shocked to see how pale Harry had gone.

'Yes, he's fine. Fully recovered, thanks to the guys at the hospital. It just made me think, that's all. About if he'd died.' She stopped and clenched her teeth to stop herself from crying. 'I felt so guilty over the years, and I realised that he could have died without ever knowing about you, and you would never have known him.'

'Dad never told me a thing; I guess it wasn't his place. I'm so sorry, Annabel, that must have been awful. That's why you called me?'

'I'd had a little to drink. I guess I was a bit of a mess once the adrenalin wore off. I wanted you there.' She pressed her lips together.

'You wanted me there?' he echoed. His grip on her hand tightened. 'I'm sorry. It must have been hard. I wish I had been there. For all of it. I can't imagine how scary it must have been for you.'

She looked across at Harry, and he was white, his face a picture of pain.

'Hey, it's okay. It was tough, but we got through it. I guess I had a bit of latent rage afterwards, and I had a drink or five when I got home—'

'Rage?'

He was looking right at her now, his lips almost bloodless.

'Yeah, you know. Life's a cruel mistress, and I think I got mad. At myself more than anything. I couldn't help him and I felt powerless. Even with everything we do in this job, I couldn't do much but just be there.'

'I bet that was more than enough for Aidan. It's just what I would have wanted.'

She gave him a little smile and looked away. 'I was just so glad he came through it. You'd never know it happened now, to look at him. It's like a bad dream.'

She was downplaying it; he knew she would. He'd known as soon as he'd heard her voice on that voicemail that she was in pain, that something was wrong with his girl. He'd almost called her back so many times, but he knew a phone call just wouldn't cut it, and for once he'd listened to his dad. He could tell she'd been drinking, and he didn't want her to take those words back. He'd wanted to be in front of her, even if it was only for her to take it back and tell him to leave again. He needed to be there, explain things. The truth was, since being cancer-free and getting the all-clear, he'd just been…waiting. For what he didn't know, until he'd got that call. Just hearing her voice told him to return home, and he wasn't done yet.

Now just wasn't the time to blindside her with a confession of his own. He couldn't tell her now; he couldn't risk shutting her down when she was finally starting to open up. He thought about the time when he was sick. When he'd wanted nothing more than her by his side, as selfish as he thought that notion was. Now, he saw that his actions had released her from caring for him, from derailing her life, but it had robbed them of so much time together. Time together that they might never have had. Still might never have, given her mistrust of him. The thought added another band of guilt around his heart. He'd believed he was setting her free to live her life, but he'd just missed out on being a family instead.

'I'm sorry about not being there, and I understand the rage you felt.'

Cancer was a silent stealer of many, many things. It might not have taken his life, but it had changed it forever in so many ways.

He took another bite of his lunch, wanting to choose his words as best he could. 'If I had known about Aidan, I would never have wanted to leave him. Leave either of you.'

'I know,' she retorted, surprising him. 'That's why I didn't tell you when I found out. You wanted that new life, and I didn't want to interfere with that. I want to listen to what you have to say, Harry, I just don't have the strength quite yet. And I might get mad and punch you in the face. It would make it awkward at work.' She flashed him a rueful grin, and his heart almost popped out of his chest.

Ah, Annie. You can never be mean for long. Not without feeling the need to cushion the blow. If someone robbed your purse in the street, you would find a way to give him a backstory. A reason why that person needed your money more than you did.

'So you covered for me, had our child, looked after my dad, and then got mad at me years later after a Chardonnay?'

She looked at him for a long moment and then started to laugh. A slightly manic laugh that made Harry's heart swell.

'I missed that laugh.'

'It was whisky, not some chick drink, and yeah, you missed a lot.' The laughter stopped then, and her smile faded. She was already checking her watch, but Harry didn't want the moment to pass.

'I know I did, but I came back. I'm here for good now.' He flashed her his very best Harry smile, the one that she never could resist. Till now, it seemed, judging from her unamused facial expression. 'I know that we're not in a good place, but I think with me being back we can—'

He wanted to keep talking, to tell her that he'd come back for her, unable to think about anything else since she'd called, but she was already shaking her head.

'There is no "we", Harry. I know I told you about Aidan, but I'm not about to uproot our lives for you when you might not even be here in a few months.'

'The job's permanent, Annie.'

She flinched at his use of her shortened name, but he kept going.

She is my Annie.

'I came here to stay. I'm looking for a place. Hell, if I'd been here any sooner I would have bought our dream house. I've left Dubai for good, Annabel, and I do want to see Aidan.

We have a lot to talk about. I'll wait till you're ready, but I mean what I say. I'm here. For good. For you both.'

She banged on the side window in frustration, and he fell silent. He'd pushed too far. He steeled himself for the punch in the face she'd joked about. Hell, he would take it if it meant getting closer to her.

'I don't think so, Harry. Can you imagine how upsetting it will be for him? I can't do it to the poor boy. He doesn't have much family; I can't risk it. He's still getting back into school, into his routine.' She almost blurted out about the move but stopped herself just in time.

'You don't have to risk anything. I'm his dad; I would never hurt him.'

Annabel snorted, throwing the rest of her sandwich back into her bag and sanitising her hands. 'You don't even know him, Harry! He doesn't know you're his dad!'

'Whose fault is that?'

'Yours! You left me there like an idiot that day. What was I supposed to do—hop on a plane with a baby bump and surprise you?'

'That would have been better than how I found out, yes, but no, I—'

'This is pointless,' she snapped at him, so hard she almost showed him her teeth like a cornered animal. 'You don't think I feel guilty enough, lying to everyone all this time? Lying to my son? Lunch is over anyway. You ready?'

Harry felt his eyes roll back in his head. 'I don't want to fall out.'

'Really? Well, you could have fooled me, Harrison.'

Damn it. She full-named me again. A sure-fire sign that she's mightily hacked off with me.

'We have to work together and that's hard enough, okay? I can't deal with anything else right now. I have a lot on, and I don't want Aidan upset.'

Harry stared straight ahead as she took the wrappers and walked out of the ambulance to put them in the nearby waste bin. She'd looked as if she wanted to take the door off with the slam she gave it, and he watched her as she stomped back over, her lips constantly moving. She was talking to herself, as she always used to when she was worked up. He knew this girl—this woman—so well, and being near her after all these years felt like torture. He just wanted to take her into his arms, tell her his truth. Not that he could now, not after the conversation they'd just shared. He could tell that reliving that memory had affected her, and he wanted to pick a better moment than when they'd just fought.

He'd give anything to see her light up again. Light up when she saw him. The smile she used to give him when he walked into a room never failed to floor him, make him want to thank his lucky stars that she loved him. Instead, she got back into the cab and, without even looking his way, she put them back on work duty. A call came in seconds later, and they were off. By the time the last call came in, any chance to restart their conversation seemed lost.

'Ambulance seventeen, you're the closest to this call. Woman, thirty-six, chest pains.'

Harry took down the details and Annabel

threw on the sirens and lights and they raced to the scene.

'Any history on this patient?' Harry asked, building up the best picture they could before arriving on scene.

'No, fit and healthy otherwise. The patient has been suffering stress of late and be aware she has an infant with her. No family to call.'

'Got it,' Harry replied. 'Two minutes ETA.'

They pulled up outside the neat house, where a woman was sitting on the doorstep, slumped over, the front door behind her wide open. They could hear crying, and next to where the woman was sitting on the front step there was a pram which was moving from side to side with the exertions of the scream-ing baby inside.

'Go!' Annabel shouted the second they pulled up, turning off the engine and yank-ing the handbrake up. She and Harry ran to the patient, kit bags on their backs. An-nabel ran straight to the woman, who was now unconscious and blue. 'She's not breath-ing, Harry!' They laid the woman down on the hallway carpet, calling out to any occupants in the house, even though they knew she was alone, hoping that someone might just have come to the woman's aid. The baby was screaming in the pram, and Annabel found no pulse. 'She's not breathing. I think it's a heart attack.' She checked the patient's airway, loosening her clothing and supporting her head. 'Starting CPR!'

Harry rushed to bring the pram indoors, the outside temperature dropping now. Checking at lightning speed, he ascertained that the baby was no more than six months old, was well looked after, just hungry and a little cold. He parked the pram at the bottom of the stairs and watched as Annabel pumped the mother's chest. Checking for a pulse again, she shook her head. 'Defibrillator!'

Harry ran to get what they needed, Annabel pulling off the clothing and getting ready to shock the patient. Harry updated the station on the patient, taking the baby in his arms to stop her crying. She snuggled into the warmth of his body, stopping crying almost immediately.

'Come on, Diane,' Annabel said to the woman

as she got everything ready, her hands moving with precise speed. 'Don't you die in front of your beautiful daughter. Come on! Clear!'

She pressed the paddles to the woman's chest, and her body jerked up with the movement. Annabel checked her pulse again, putting the paddles aside.

'We have a pulse!' Diane gasped for air, coughing and murmuring as she came to. 'Diane, Diane, it's okay. We're from the ambulance service. We're here to help; we need to get you to hospital.' Harry had already laid the baby back down in the pram and was racing to get a stretcher. They hooked her up to monitor her heart, and Annabel made her lie back down when she tried to get up.

'Izzy?' she asked. 'Where's my Izzy?'

'She's right here,' Harry said from behind her. They lifted her onto the stretcher and strapped her in, Harry picking up the baby and letting her mother see her. 'Do you have milk in the changing bag?' Diane nodded weakly, and Harry picked it up off the back of the pram. 'Let's get you both in. Do you have anyone who could look after the baby?'

Diane shook her head, crying now. Annabel gave her some pain medication, and she settled a little. 'No,' Diane said weakly. 'My husband left me. He's selling the house. He left me for someone else. I've been so stressed. What happened?'

Annabel took the woman's hand in her gloved one, leaning in so Diane would stay settled. 'We think you had a mild heart attack, Diane, but we have some of the best doctors in the country waiting to help you. We'll take Izzy with us, okay?' The woman nodded, crying again now. Checking the monitors, both paramedics were happy to see that her stats were coming back up. She was out of the woods for now, but they needed to act fast.

'I just felt a bit ill. I thought it was heartburn. How did I have a heart attack?'

Harry, leading the stretcher out of the house, the baby quiet and settled in his arms, gave Diane a comforting smile while Annabel checked the house over quickly and locked up. She put the keys in the changing bag on Harry's shoulder and within minutes they were heading off. Harry offered to drive, and Annabel was glad. She didn't want to leave the poor woman alone. She'd grabbed the detachable car seat from the pram, and she strapped the baby into the seat in the back of the cab, wrapping a blanket around her. She was now starting to stir, reminded of her hungry belly.

'Do you want to call your husband? Anyone?'

'I only have Izzy. It was just the three of us. I thought it would always be that way. Don't call him, please.'

Diane shook her head, and Annabel didn't press the matter. Harry closed the doors, but not before he squeezed Annabel's shoulder.

'Good job there,' he told her.

'Back at you,' she said, meaning every word. 'Drive fast.'

Harry winked at her before he closed the doors, and she turned her attention back to the woman. They'd got there in time, but she knew that the image of the new mother, slumped and alone, the baby crying next to her, wouldn't leave her for a long time. She had people, but once she locked her doors in the evening it was just her and Aidan. The thought of something happening to her was something she tried not to dwell on, but it was there just the same. Seeing Harry hold the baby girl in his strong arms hadn't helped either. He'd never held Aidan like that, and she felt the pain of moments lost once more, and the crushing guilt of her decision. She'd taken things away from him too. Moments they would never get to have. They blue lighted it all the way to the hospital, and they didn't leave till the social worker turned up to help with the baby. Diane was going to be fine, but she had a long hard road ahead and she would need help to get there.

When they both got back into the ambulance some time later, they sat for a moment.

'I hope they'll be okay. She looked terrified.'

'She's a new mum going through a lot already. Hopefully the dad will come through for her.'

Aidan's jaw tightened, and she patted his leg. He reached for her hand and held it there, under his.

'If you ever need me like that, you'd call, right?'

She looked across at him, his features shadowed in the fast fading light outside.

'Of course,' she replied. 'It's one of my biggest fears. Not being well enough to take care of him. If I needed you, I'd call.'

He lifted her hand to his mouth and kissed it once. The shivers that ran down her arm could have been from the cold of the evening, but she knew it was more than that.

'Thank you,' he said. 'I'll always be here. Let's get signed off, eh? It's been a day.' He didn't let go of her hand the whole time, and for once she didn't object to his attentions.

They pulled into the station, sorted their jobs out and went in to clock off. Harry waved to some familiar faces, most of whom looked back at him open-mouthed. Word had spread about his return. He had expected as much.

Annabel went on ahead, her shoulders hunched. She'd probably seen the looks he was getting too. It was hardly likely to get her to let her guard down. He wanted to tell them all to mind their own business.

'God, I wish they wouldn't gawp,' she said at the side of him, while his face set into an irritated scowl. 'I'd better get my paperwork done.' He watched her leave. He could almost hear her defences clanging back up into place. Looking back down the corridor, he made a point of staring the onlookers out. Most of them had the good sense to look away, scattering like autumn leaves in the wind. Spotting a friendly familiar face, he started to smile.

'Purdie!' he said out loud, loud enough for everyone to hear. 'You are a sight for sore eyes.'

Purdie came running over, enveloping him in a perfume-soaked hug. Harry was taken aback for a second but wrapped his arms around his old friend. Their old friend.

'So,' she said when she finally released

him. 'Finally saw sense and came home, eh? Good to be back?'

Annabel's office door slammed behind them, and the remaining onlookers moved on. Purdie raised a thick dark brow at him, nodding towards the door. 'That well, eh?' She pulled him in for another hug and as he leaned in she whispered in his ear, 'Give her time, Harry; it's been a bit of a year for her.'

He opened his mouth in shock. 'How do you know what I'm thinking?'

Purdie slapped him on the arm as they pulled away from each other. She straightened his uniform like a proud mother hen. 'I know you kids, remember? You're made for each other. Just give her space.'

Harry pulled a face. 'I sort of think that was the issue in the first place.'

He got another slap for that one.

'I know, and you upset a lot of people around here, but some things just need to be done. I know you meant well. Life's messy, Harrison Carter.' She gave him her sternest look as she turned to go home, bag and coat in hand. 'It's time to clear up that mess, once and for all. You good, all healed?' She said this more softly, and he frowned at her question. Purdie was one of the few people who knew about his earlier diagnosis—she'd been working in Oncology at the time.

Was he all healed? Physically, sure, but the heart took a little longer to mend. Especially when a huge piece of it was missing.

'I'm good,' he said eventually, and she left happy. Harry found himself alone in the corridor, staring at Annabel's office door as though it was the entrance to heaven and he'd been hell-raising half his life. He could walk through that door right now, tell her the whole truth about why he'd left, convince her that he *was* here to stay. Make her believe him, that his running days were over for good. That finding out about Aidan had made him so happy, so utterly happy.

His childhood sweetheart had loved him enough, even after what he did, to raise his child and keep his name out of it. She could have done a million different things to strike back at him, and understandably so, but she hadn't. She'd even looked after his dad when his own son had never really known how. He knew he didn't deserve her, but he wanted her to look at him the way she used to. As if the sun and moon rose and fell with him. The way that he still looked at her. When she wasn't looking, anyway.

He stopped in front of the door, his hand raised in a fist, ready to knock. He could hear her moving about inside; she was so close now, just at the other side of the wood. He wanted to tell her how he felt, why he'd left—everything. Earlier it hadn't been the right moment, but he had to make one. He couldn't keep it inside him any longer. He wanted her to know the real reason he'd left. That leaving had torn him apart just as much as it had her. He wanted to meet his son too, but he understood why she was reluctant to let him. He'd destroyed her life back then, and he couldn't blame her for wanting to avoid that all over again. She was still there though, under her new tougher exterior. He knew she was still there; he just needed her to trust him again.

Pushing his hands into his pockets to stop himself from banging on the door and declaring his intentions, he summoned the energy to walk away. He needed her to see that he wasn't going anywhere. He needed to prove to his family that he was back, and he wasn't going anywhere again. Which reminded him; he had something to take care of himself. After he'd told his father about his cancer, Abe had implored him to get checked over now he was in the UK. Ever the GP, but he had a point. He needed to make sure he stayed well, so he could finally, after so long, claim his life back. He just hoped that Annabel would be interested in his plans. He couldn't help but get the feeling that it might just be too late.

He had almost reached his rental car when his phone buzzed with a text. *Annabel.* His heart thudded loud and hard in his ears as he opened it up.

Aidan is due a visit to Abe's. If you are there at seven tonight, you can meet him. My terms.

He doesn't know, and I want it kept that way, for now at least. You get one chance, Harry. Don't blow it.

Harry didn't even remember the drive home. When he walked into his dad's house later that evening, his face flushed with happiness, arms filled with shopping bags, Abe just raised a brow at him from his easy chair.

'You got a date?' The television was on in the background, a steaming mug of tea by his side. It felt as if he'd just come home from school; the wave of nostalgia hit Harry as soon as he walked in.

'Annabel said that I could meet Aidan, not as his dad yet, but still. I got a few things on the way home, snacks and a few games.'

Abe chuckled. 'We have food, you know, and games.' He looked as if he was enjoying all this.

'I know, but I wanted to make an effort, you know. They'll be here soon. What do you normally do?'

'Well, we eat and watch a bit of television.

If it's nice we have a walk. Aidan generally takes the lead. He's a good kid. You make that appointment yet?' Their liquor cabinet talk had really been a bare-all for the two Carter men. His dad had cried and held his son close. It had thawed them a little, but now the doctor in him was getting bossy already.

'Not yet, but I will, I promise. Time got away from me today. Dad, has Aidan never asked you if you were his real grandfather, or asked about his father?'

Abe looked away then, muttering something about changing the subject and asking silly questions, and Harry knew why. 'I get it—I left. I just wondered, that's all. I'll just put all this away. Is Annabel staying too?'

He'd realised, walking around the aisles in the shop, that she hadn't said in her text whether it was just Aidan who was visiting. That had sent him into a spiral as he'd considered where she could be going. A date, maybe? He didn't dwell on that for too long; he didn't want to think about another man raising his son or loving his girl. She'd given no indication that she even was dating. He knew he had no real rights here, but the second Annabel had told him about their son, before even, he hadn't been able to stop the fire he felt inside him. The same fire he'd felt when he'd received that voicemail. He just needed to find a way to stoke the embers in Annabel's heart. If enough still remained. He'd told her he'd been on a few dates, which was true, but he wanted her to know that no one had measured up to her. Not that he'd been looking. He'd always just felt as if he was hers, in a weird way.

'Nope,' Abe said easily, his focus already back on his TV show. 'She's got a lot of work to do at the house.'

'The house?' Aidan checked. 'You mean her mum's old place?'

Abe looked over the top of his glasses at his son.

'No. She bought the dream house, Harry. You two really need to talk.'

Harry remembered them passing that house today, seeing the sold sign out front. Another cog clicked into place. She'd brushed him off when he'd spoken about it. He'd assumed it was too painful to think of. He realised now she'd been avoiding the truth.

'She never said.'

Abe's glasses bumped up his nose, taken along for the ride by his raised brows.

'I wonder why. Not exactly an open book these days, is she? It's a bit of a shack, to be honest; she has her work cut out for her. Especially working full-time, and with Aidan. But that's Annabel, right? She's never shied away from anything.'

Harry's shoulders slumped and he headed to the kitchen to get ready for Aidan's arrival. 'I get it, Dad,' he said half to himself, half to the occupant of the other room. 'She's amazing and I screwed up. I get it.' He pulled out one of the board games he'd bought, one he'd enjoyed as a kid. 'I don't have a clue what I'm doing. I'm not a father. You don't need to fill me in. I'm all up to speed on my failings.'

'I didn't mean it like that. Don't be such a prickly pear. I get why you left now, you know that. You think I had it all figured out when you came along?' Abe was in the kitchen doorway now, and Harry sat down on one of the breakfast bar stools. He felt so damn tired. 'When your mum passed, I had no clue. I regret a lot of things, son, but never you. I don't always understand you, but I know you loved Annabel back then.' He walked over, patting Harry's hand as he took a seat. 'And now, I'm betting. She hasn't exactly been busy on the man front either, not for lack of her friends trying over the years. Don't beat yourself up for not being a father. You didn't know, and you can't be mad at Annabel for that either. You're a brand-new dad. It's up to you now what sort of father you are.'

'I'm not mad at her.' Harry felt the need to defend Annabel even now. 'I left you all. She did what she thought was best.' He thought of how he might have taken the news if she had called back then. He'd been living in another country, not working at saving lives but fighting for his own. He wouldn't have been much help, and knowing his family were so far away would have killed him harder than the cancer wanted to. He'd won that battle, and now he needed to fight for his life once more. The one he'd never wanted to leave behind in the first place. He just had even more to fight for than he'd thought, and it made him all the more determined to do it.

Abe nodded in agreement. 'She did, and keeping that secret cost her a lot. You know how people talk. They love a bit of dirty laundry, a juicy bit of gossip. She tarnished her own reputation a little, so as not to take any more shine off yours. She's loyal to a fault. If you really want her back, son, you need to prove it to her. And Aidan.'

'No pressure then.'

Abe laughed, patting his hand again. 'You can do it, Harry. I'll help.' Reaching his arm across, he hugged his son to him and dropped a kiss on the top of his head. 'I'm glad you came home.'

Harry hugged his father to him, marvelling at the change in him. Maybe time and distance, along with the truth, had healed some of their old niggles. An ointment on old wounds.

'Me too, Dad,' Harry said honestly. 'Me too. Let's get ready for the little guy.'

CHAPTER THREE

ANNABEL PARKED HER car outside Abe's house and looked out of the window, a deep sigh leaving her as she steeled herself for this momentous event.

'What's wrong, Mummy?' Aidan, sitting in the back seat with a pair of headphones half hanging off his ears, took off his seatbelt and wrapped his little arm around her shoulder. She could hear his favourite anime cartoons playing through the ear buds attached to his tablet. She turned and gave him her best 'everything's okay' smile.

'Nothing, kiddo, just a long day. You know I can't stay tonight, right? I have a guy coming to the house to look at the back garden.' She wanted to get it overhauled. It had been a lovely garden once, but it had got too much for the previous owner. Annabel had big plans. A patio so her station family could come for barbecues while the kids played on the play equipment she knew Aidan would love. She wanted a little vegetable patch so she and Aidan could grow their own food, something to do together. Her mother had always wanted one, and the balcony of their old flat had always had something growing, every bit of space used cleverly for home-grown fruit and vegetables. Doing it together, like she used to do with her own mum, would be family time well spent.

Aidan was so proud of his mum for the job she did; he was a great kid. Their quality time meant a lot, and having a garden was a huge plus to the house. The landscape gardener had been kind enough to meet her after work, though the timing could have been better. Leaving Aidan with Abe and Harry was so weird; she couldn't get her head around it. After the call today though, with Diane and baby Izzy, she figured Aidan knowing Harry might be a good thing after all.

'Listen, Granddad has someone living with

him at the moment. Remember the photos of his son that you see around the house?'

Aidan nodded at her slowly, his eyes wide. 'He came home from far away? Really?'

'He did, so he's going to be there tonight. That okay?' She brushed his fringe away from his little face, the freckles across his nose matching her own. 'He's nice, and he works with me now, so you might be seeing him around for a bit.'

'Because Uncle Tom is getting me some cousins?'

Aidan had always loved being around people. He'd asked for a baby brother or sister for the last three Christmases. She was hoping that once the house was done she could get him a pet, stop the awkward questions. Tom and Lloyd having babies around would be great too, and she was looking forward to babysitting for them. She'd loved being a mum to Aidan right from the start, even though it was hard and lonely at times.

She felt the old feelings of resentment towards Harry creep into her thoughts, and she pushed them away. The last thing she wanted was for Aidan to pick up on any tension, and she found that the anger wasn't as strong as before. It helped that he'd told her he had only been on a couple of dates, but was that true? She had always wondered whether he had met someone over there. It had been a long time, and he was a hot single man. She could see what a catch he would have been over there, single and available. Was it really just a few dates?

'That's right, so Harry has come to work with me now, in Tom's job.'

Aidan gave her a little side look. 'Is he your best friend? Where has he been? What does he look like? Does he have a girlfriend? Is he staying forever?'

Annabel laughed, getting out of the car and opening Aidan's door. 'Wow, what's with all the questions today? Let's get you inside, I'm going to be late at this rate. I won't be too long, and I'm on a day off soon. We can do something. Cinema, maybe?'

Aidan nodded distractedly, already running through the flowerbeds to Abe's front door.

'Hey, wait up!'

The door opened just as he reached it, and Aidan crashed straight into Harry's legs.

'Hey, hello!' Harry caught him and righted him on his feet. 'You must be Aidan. I'm Harry.'

Annabel saw the shake in Harry's hand as he held it out to her son. *Their son.* Aidan stood frozen for a long minute before putting his hand into Harry's. Annabel felt as if she was going to pass out, but she held it together. Aidan turned and beamed at her. She tried not to catch Harry's eye, but they met anyway. She had half expected to see anger there, or fear, but all she saw was his happiness. He mouthed 'Thank you' to her, but she didn't respond. She felt as though she was rooted to the spot.

'Aidan, be good, okay? I'll be back soon.'

'Bye, Mum. Granddad, I'm here!' He was off indoors, leaving the pair of them standing at opposite ends of the path.

'Thanks for bringing him. Do you want some supper saving? I think we went a little overboard on the food.'

She opened her mouth to say no, but stopped

herself. She needed to get on with him. She needed to squash down her feelings from the past, all of them. Good and bad.

'You know what, that would actually be great. I haven't eaten since lunch. I won't be more than a couple of hours.'

Harry nodded, his lopsided grin making him look like the boy she'd once known. 'Great. See you soon.' She was about to open her car door when he called out to her, 'Annie?'

She turned, leaning against her car door to face him. In the faded daylight, he was framed by the light coming from inside the house. She squashed down the feelings of attraction that stirred within her.

Why does he have to be so darned cute? I'm pretty sure that there should be some kind of rule for this kind of thing. Once someone stomps on your heart, they should suddenly lose all charm for the person who was left. He had to come back all put together and hot. Why can't he be fat, or balding? An extra chin or two wouldn't go amiss.

'Will you meet me tomorrow? We're both off shift.'

The fact that he now knew her timetable should have irked her, but they were working partners now, needing to be on the same shifts while his probationary period was ongoing. Annabel was torn over it. Did she want him to stay after? Would he want to stay after? It was exhausting trying to work out how she felt, to guess what the future might hold. So she did what she did best. She protected her heart.

'I have a bit of a full day, Harry; you know what time off is like. I have a ton of stuff to do—'

'At the dream house?' He said it softly. Not an accusation, a soft question. Annabel felt her whole body deflate. She leaned against her car for a moment, steadying herself.

'I don't want to fight, Harry.'

'You said you would listen to me. I just want to talk.'

He was heading down the path towards her before she could react, pulling the door shut behind him. He stopped right in front of her. The proximity of him made her heart flutter in her chest. She could just reach out and touch him, right now. Her hands tingled with the urge to touch her fingers to his chest. She used to love to run her fingers through his hair before pulling his mouth down to hers. She crossed her arms for lack of anything else to do with them. In the same moment, he shifted from one foot to the other and pushed his hands into his back pockets.

Was he feeling it too? It felt like a lot more than muscle memory.

She ached to bridge the gap between them, but it wasn't her who had put it there in the first place.

'I don't want to fight either. You asked me to come home, remember?'

'Six months ago, when I was tipsy and upset! Where were you then? Breaking some other girl's heart?'

Wow, where did that come from? Aidan's girlfriend question had obviously stuck in her mind.

'What? No! I had a contract, I told you. I worked my notice and left the same day. I came back. We've been over this. I told you the truth. I didn't want to do this over the phone. Why are you mad again?' He ran his hand through his hair, pulling at it a little in frustration. 'We need to talk about it all, about why I left.'

Annabel almost relented right there and then. He was offering to tell her why he'd left her that day, to raise his secret son alone and pick up the pieces of her life. She knew he hadn't known about the baby—hell, she was a trained paramedic and she hadn't even realised she was pregnant herself. She'd lain awake for so many nights, gazing down at her ever-expanding belly and wondering what Harry would have done if he'd known back then. If she'd called him on any of those nights.

The fact was, though, it was in the past. Some things you couldn't just take back. She was glad he knew now. The knot in the pit of her stomach had almost fossilised over the last eight years, and now the secret was out she felt lighter. Stronger too. She wasn't quite that panicked, worried mother she'd been six months ago. It had been a moment of weakness and, no matter what he said, she had spent all of Aidan's life believing Harry to be an utter cad. Nothing he told her would change that, and it was yet another reason to keep him at arm's length. She didn't want to betray that girl at the airport, the sacrifices they had all had to make since. It was painful enough to remember those early days. She had blocked a lot of them out. She would never have survived otherwise. It had just been the three of them for so long. Her, Abe and Aidan. While Harry had lived it up on the other side of the world as a ghost to those who loved him, a breaker of hearts.

'Tell me something first,' she said quietly. He leaned in a little, and she found herself leaning further away from him, pushing herself against her car. He made her head swim even now, but she needed to get this out.

'Anything,' he breathed. She clenched her teeth and looked him square in the eye.

'I did want to listen to what you have to say. I do. But answer this one thing for me. Whatever you have to tell me, will it erase what you did that day? Leaving me standing there like an idiot with my suitcases, and walking away from me? Making everyone we know wonder what they had done wrong.'

He reeled as though her words had slapped him across his chiselled features. 'Well, no, but if you j—'

'Then I don't need to know. Aidan is your son, you wanted to meet him—well, here he is.' She gestured with her hand towards the house, and spotted Abe watching them from behind the curtain. When he saw her looking he melted away and the curtains were pulled shut. 'Go meet him. He's a great kid. He will probably have a million questions for you. He's always wanted to go and see other countries. With one thing and another, we've not had a lot of time for holidays.' He winced, and she pushed down her sarcasm once more. 'I'm sorry, I really have to go.'

'To the dream house, yeah? You never answered me before.'

Great. Was everything about her life on show now, for him to comment on? She could tell he wasn't about to let this drop.

'Yes, the dream house. It's part of a different dream now, though. One for me and Aidan. I'll see you at work, okay?'

She left him standing by the kerb, hands on his hips. As she drove away, she willed herself not to look back at him in the mirror, but she found herself watching him as she drove away. When he was out of sight she brushed a tear away from her cheek and willed herself to pull it together. The way he'd looked at her was killing her.

Not for the first time, she found herself wondering if he would stay. What would London have to offer over Dubai for a man like him? Abe wasn't sick; he was still as fit as a fiddle and as sharp as a drawer full of knives. He'd not come back through obligation.

He said he'd come back because of her, but whenever she thought about thawing enough to speak to him properly, to hash out the last few years, Aidan's little face popped into her head. The way she'd felt in that airport. The years of people asking her about her son's father. All the times she had covered for him, making herself look worse in order for the people in their lives not to hate Harry, to tell him about his son. Any one of them could have got in touch with Harry to tell him about Aidan, to berate him for leaving them both. She had never wanted that, nor had she wanted to be a charity case either. She knew him well enough to know that he would have come home to do the right thing. The right thing by her, the woman he said he loved—but not enough to treat her better in the first place.

She'd chosen her path, and even though Aidan had had tears over the years about not having a dad like most of his school friends, they'd done just fine. She wasn't about to change that. Not on the strength of a few days, or because she knew how nostalgic she felt when Harry was around her. The thought of Aidan getting to know his father and then getting an airport goodbye like she did was enough to keep her driving away from him, and not driving back into his arms. What if he had run back home to hide from another woman he had left, back in Dubai? Could she trust him, really?

She had felt her resolve weakening when he

was there right in front of her, but their compatibility had never been the problem. Him leaving her high and dry was the issue, and she just knew that she would never survive that again. When he told her the reason he'd left, and she knew he would, it would either make her hate him forever or make it that bit harder not to fall completely back in love with him. Given his eagerness to tell her and the way he'd looked at her, she was guessing it would be the latter. She needed a minute to prepare at least. She wasn't a young girl any more. She had other people to consider.

By the time she pulled up outside her house, giving a wave to the waiting gardener, all her tears had been shed and she had composed herself once more. Yet another piece of gauze wrapped around her shattered heart.

She wanted to know.

As Harry watched the love of his life drive away he thought his heart would snap in two. She still didn't fully trust him, and that thought was one that he could barely bear. Slapping his hand to his forehead the second her car turned out of sight, he kept his back to the house and willed himself to pull it together. He ran his hands down his face, surprised when they came away wet with his tears. He felt lower than a snake's belly and, after the day he'd left her, he didn't think it was possible to feel any worse. The light had gone out of his Annie, and he was the reason.

Pulling himself together, he turned back to the house. It was time to get to know his son and prove to his mother that he was still the man she'd once adored. He knew it would be a battle, but Harrison Carter was ready to stand and fight with everything he had.

'Hey,' he called when he walked back into the house. Aidan was playing a board game with Abe, rolling the dice as if his little life depended on it. Abe looked at him expectantly, and Harry shook his head. Abe scowled, his shoulders sagging.

'Stubborn,' he said to no one in particular. Harry's mouth twitched.

'Mum says I'm stubborn too.' Aidan was looking straight at Harry now, and Abe stood up from his seat.

'I'll put the kettle on. I bought extra marshmallows for the hot chocolate too.'

'Did she now?' Harry went to sit on the couch next to his son, taking the opportunity to continue the conversation.

'Yep. Are you really stubborn too?'

Grinning, Harry nodded, taking in every little detail of the child in front of him. 'I've been told that before, so yes, I'm stubborn.'

Aidan grinned. 'I knew it. Want to play?'

He offered Harry the dice, and he took them gratefully. 'There's nothing I'd like better.'

CHAPTER FOUR

DRIVING BACK HOME the next day after the hectic rush of the morning school run, Annabel played back the previous evening in her head. Aidan had crashed out on the couch at Abe's house, which meant that she took her supper to go, wanting to get Aidan into his own bed. Harry had carried him out to the car and not pressed for anything else. He'd closed the car door, leaned in and brushed his lips against her cheek, then simply walked back inside. She'd been left leaning against her car door, feeling as if her face was on fire from the touch of his lips, and confused about his sudden mood change. Had he given up already?

This morning Aidan had been full of Harry talk, about how awesome he was, how much Granddad had laughed, how rubbish Harry was at Scrabble. She had a feeling they'd had a lot of fun and she wished she could have seen them together. Seeing Harry striding across Abe's front path, their sleeping son in his arms, could quite easily have been her favourite calendar photo for the next, oh, ten years. He was so natural with him, and when he'd leant in close and kissed her on the cheek she'd almost turned and sought his lips. By the time she'd argued with herself about the merits of leaving or grabbing his face and kissing the life out of him, he'd turned and left, leaving her shell-shocked and standing on the front lawn, clinging to her car like a shipwrecked sailor clinging to a piece of driftwood. She thanked her lucky stars it was their day off and she could recover. Maybe even take a cold shower.

Pulling up in front of her house, she frowned when she noticed a car parked outside. She wasn't expecting any workmen today, and the landscape gardener wasn't due to start for a few days. She thought the car looked familiar on the second look, and when she parked up and the car door opened she knew why.

'Morning!' Harry was standing there, dressed in a pair of jeans and a white T-shirt that made his tanned skin look all the more alluring. She could make out the contours of his muscular body under the thin white cotton. His hair was neat and styled and he was holding two coffees in his hands and a rather large brown paper bag. 'Aidan let slip that you were decorating your lounge today, so I thought I'd come to help.'

In contrast to the well put together Adonis before her, Annabel felt like fresh roadkill. She'd scraped her hair back into a messy bun that morning, she had pancake batter down her hooded sweatshirt from making Aidan breakfast and she was currently wearing her paint-splattered decorating joggers. She wanted the ground to swallow her up.

'I…er…' She could smell the coffee now as they gravitated towards each other. She scrambled for a response that would make him leave but gave in when her stomach rumbled. She thought back to last night and smiled at him. His face lit up when he saw it and broke out in a sexy grin.

Oh, Harry.

'It depends. What's in the bag?'

'Bacon rolls with red sauce,' he teased, raising his eyebrows. 'You eaten?'

She threw him a grin of her own. 'I'm starved.'

He gestured towards the house. 'Breakfast for a tour? I brought some dust sheets from Dad too; he said you might need some.'

They walked up to the house together and Annabel watched him take it in as she unlocked the door and motioned for him to come inside.

'It looks so different. I can't believe you bought the place.'

Annabel laughed, thinking of the time warp she had sunk every penny into. 'I could hardly keep the old decor of the place as it was. Maud was lovely, but she didn't really bother with interior design. I found newspapers under the floorboards older than my grandfather. It's taken a lot of work to even get to this stage.'

They were standing next to each other in the hallway, and once more she felt the pull of him. They were here, in the house they'd always sworn they'd buy together, where they'd raise a family while saving the world one patient at a time. They were here, and so were the details, but the reality was far different.

I know he feels this too.

One look at him, and she knew. He was feeling everything she was, including the urge to just reach for the other and breathe them in. She felt so thirsty for him, and he was the one man that she couldn't drink in. It would never be just a sip, and then she'd be lost forever.

Not forever. He'll probably be gone by Christmas.

Annabel wasn't sure whether it was her voice she heard in her head or her mother's.

She saw his gaze fall on a photo of her and Aidan, taken at Aidan's last birthday party. It was sitting in the hallway on top of a box of stuff she couldn't unpack yet.

'I bet,' he replied, moving through the hallway and into the lounge. The builders had knocked through to the dining room and freshly plastered; it looked huge now. Annabel pinched herself every time she walked through the door. It was awful living in a building site, but the space was well worth it. Every week she saw her house come together, and it was worth all the dust and the hassle. She couldn't wait to just come home and enjoy her time off with Aidan. Barbecues in the garden with his friends coming around, Abe coming for Sunday dinner. Maybe she would even invite Harry too, if he was still around.

'Annabel, did you hear me?'

She realised that Harry was talking to her, and she followed him through to the lounge.

'Sorry, I was miles away. What?'

He was looking at the paint tins and rollers that were sitting off to one side. 'This is what you're doing today?' He looked at the light grey paint colour on the side of one of the cans. 'Nice colour.'

'Thanks, yeah. I was hoping to get it done but, looking at it...' That was the only problem with a big space; it meant more work.

Harry sat down on the floor and patted the

floor beside him. 'We'll get it done. Eat first though, yeah?'

'We? Really?'

Harry shook his head at her. 'Annabel, this is getting old now. I'm here. For you, for Aidan. I'm not going anywhere. Just let me help, okay?'

Annabel sighed, taking a seat next to him.

'What, no rebuttal?' he asked, amusement clear in his voice and the twitch in his lip.

'What can I say?' she countered, holding out her hand for him to shake. 'A girl will do anything for bacon.'

After they'd demolished everything he'd brought they got to work. Well, Harry just started opening the paint cans and laying out the dust sheets and Annabel followed his lead. She flicked on the radio and, before too long, the pair of them were rollering the walls and singing along to the music. They kept to the small talk, nothing too taxing and nothing about the past. He told her some stories from his job in Dubai, some of the best and worst cases he'd had, and she found herself telling him hers, about their colleagues and the things that had happened to the station family over the years.

'Purdie still working at the hospital then?' Harry was wiggling his bum to a Diana Ross track, his brush making precise neat strokes along the top of the freshly fitted skirting boards. 'I thought she'd have retired by now, gone home to her family.'

Annabel rolled her eyes at him. 'Not quite, not from lack of trying though. I think she's always too worried about letting her patients down; she talks about it, but then never quite follows it through. I think she might soon though; her family has changed now, expanding. You don't have anyone you miss, from Dubai?'

They ended up at the paint can at the same time, their brushes banging into each other as they both went to dip the bristles into the paint. His other hand was on hers in a second.

'I had friends, yes, good friends. We'll stay in touch. You know I was telling the truth right, about not having anyone over there?'

'I did wonder.'

His jaw flexed. 'Yeah, well, you don't have to. There wasn't anyone. Even if I had been looking, no one would have come close to you.' His hand was still on hers, his grip tightening just a little.

She swallowed hard. 'I'm a tough act to follow,' she teased back, feeling as if her skin was on fire from his touch. He took the brush from her and crossed it with his across the top of the paint can.

'I don't really care what you thought. I can't blame you for wondering. It wasn't like I hadn't imagined you with someone else, someone else making you happy. I never looked at anyone else once I met you. I know you don't trust me, but you can trust that.'

'I do.' She squeezed his hand, rubbing her thumb along the back like she always did. They'd always had a thing about hand holding. In the car, on the couch watching TV, in bed as they fell asleep. 'I know that.' Their hands were having a little reunion of their own.

Harry moved, and his mouth was on hers before she even registered the movement.

For a long, sweet, heart-pumping minute she kissed him back. She could feel his stubble on her cheek as he lowered his mouth to her neck, leaving a trail of hot salty caresses on her collarbone as he pulled her closer. He pushed the paint can to one side with his knee and lifted her up with him till their torsos touched. The feel of his body against hers ignited something in her, and she wrapped her arms around him, pulling him to her greedily. He pulled her to her feet, not once letting their lips or arms break contact. He walked her backwards towards the wall and, remembering at the last moment that it was wet with fresh paint, she pushed against him gently to stop him. He noticed and pulled away in an instant, his face pulled into a frown.

'Sorry, did I do something wrong? Do you want me to stop? I just couldn't help it. I've been wanting to kiss you since I saw you.'

She giggled, lifting a hand to smooth out his furrowed brow. 'Wet paint,' she reminded him. 'And me too.'

He smiled, his expression changing from stricken concern to happiness, and he moved his hands around her bottom, lifting her till she was straddling him, secure in his arms. They had just reached the hallway towards the bottom of the stairs when there was a loud knock at the door.

Harry had never been as upset to see a post-man in his life. Annabel jumped away from him, running to the door to answer the intrusion into their moment together.

She kissed me back. She wanted me.

The thought made his heart soar and once she had returned to him, a few little parcels and envelopes in her arms, he went to her again.

'Wait...' She stopped him in his tracks. He could see her chest heaving, just like his own. They were both smeared with spots and trails of dove-grey paint, tell-tale signs of where their hands had just been on each other's bod-ies. 'Harry, we can't.'

He could feel his shoulders sag, and a pang in his heart at her words.

'Why not? You kissed me back, Annie.'

Her face was stricken and she touched her

fingers to her lips. 'I know. I know I did but I shouldn't have. I got carried away. I think you should go.'

Harry did not want to leave. He never wanted to leave. 'No, please, Annie—'

'It's Annabel. I think you need to. We can't be alone.'

'But you said—'

'I know what I said, but it's just lust, Harry. Nostalgia. We're not those people any more; we have a son. Responsibilities.' She waggled a parcel in his direction and he saw Aidan's name on it. He had never hated the postal service before, but he sure did now, for shaking them out of the moment. He'd been so close.

'What about tomorrow, at work? We'll be alone in the ambulance. We need to talk; I have to tell you—'

'I don't want to hear that yet! You know that!'

'Why? What are you afraid of? That you'll have no reason not to be with me any more? To give this a try?' he shouted back at her, but she jumped at his tone. *Damn it.* He never wanted to make her feel like that. 'I'm sorry.

I didn't mean to shout. I don't want to go.' He motioned around him at the half-finished room. 'We need to finish this. Let me go get some lunch; we can talk then.'

She gripped the contents of her arms to her tighter and looked around her at the room. 'I only have a few hours; my friend's on school pickup. Aidan will be coming.'

'That's fine. I can be gone by then, if that's what you want. He knows we work together. It's not that unusual that I would be here, surely?'

She kept her distance from him and although he wanted to grab the post and take her into his arms, he resisted the urge.

'I don't regret the kiss. Do you?'

It took her a while to answer, and Harry held his breath for every long second while he watched her process her emotions. Eventually, she slowly shook her head. 'No, I don't, but it's just so complicated, Harry.'

She wanted it too. That made his heart skip a beat.

'I know, but I'm not going anywhere, Annie. Never again.'

'How do I know that you mean that? I never thought you'd go in the first place. I couldn't go through that again if you left, or it didn't work out. You said it wasn't working before. That could happen again.'

Harry sighed hard, all the energy leaving him. 'I know I hurt you when I left, and I didn't ever expect to do that either, believe me. I was a mess, Annie, but I'm not that person any more. A lot has changed, and knowing about Aidan…' He couldn't help but smile at the thought of his little boy. The little boy that they had made out of so much love. His little miracle baby. Made before the cancer ravaged his fertility and took away what he'd thought was his chance of ever becoming a father. 'He's amazing, Annie, and I want to be his dad more than anything. I want you, both of you. You just have to let me prove that to you.' He slowly moved towards her now, and she didn't back away. Taking the parcels and envelopes from her, he put them to one side and took her hands in his. 'And I will prove it. That I'm the partner you had before, in work and out. Will you let me?'

* * *

He was saying all the right things. The feel of his hands in hers made her nerve-endings sing, and she was still reeling from that kiss.

God, that kiss. The physical side of things had always been great, and her body was still on fire from getting a taste of him after all this time.

If they hadn't been interrupted, she was pretty sure that she wouldn't have put a stop to things. She wanted to let him in, but her previous hurt was in her head the whole time. And then there was Aidan. The poor kid had always believed that his granddad was a friend of mummy's, and his father was out of the picture. And now Harry was back, he'd met Aidan, he was supposedly here to stay, and it would be so easy. She could just let him in, back into her life and everyone else's. Give Aidan the father he had always wanted and deserved. She knew what it was like not to have one. Did she really want that for Aidan? Wasn't it why she had always turned down any offers from suitors over the years? She just couldn't seem to find the words when it came to saying yes. That airport heartbreak had become a millstone around her neck. Every time she saved a life, did well at work, aced another week of single parenting, that was what always whispered in the back of her mind.

He left you there, without even a backward glance. Everything you did up to that point and beyond, the fact that you weren't enough was always there.

It was one of the reasons she'd never bothered with dating once she'd had Aidan. Her friends, and even Abe on occasion, had tried to set her up with dates, but she'd never pulled the trigger on any of the prospective new men in her life.

Sometimes, on her worst days, when Aidan was playing up, the chores were never ending and work was full-on, she went back to that day. Sometimes she felt like whatever she did, however independent she was, she would always be that girl who vomited in the middle of the airport lounge after being left high and dry by the man who was supposed to put her before all others. BAE, indeed. One of her so-called 'friends' from work had once joked that Harry had took it to mean, *Bye, Annabel. End of.* She'd never forgotten that.

'Annie? You there?' Harry's voice pulled her back into the room and she broke the physical contact with him and turned away, kneeling by the little stack of deliveries and starting to open them up.

'Yeah, I'm here. Ham on white for me, please. The old sandwich shop around the corner's still there. I'll sort these out.'

She felt him behind her, and his feet didn't move. She concentrated on opening the next cardboard box as if her life and sanity depended on it. She couldn't trust herself to look at him, so she did what she always did. She buried it deep in her heart, away from the harsh light of day. Opening parcels and painting she could do. Major life decisions would have to wait till another day.

'I won't be long,' Harry said eventually. She could hear the rejection in his dull tone, and she closed her eyes against the sting of tears that threatened to erupt. The door closed, but when she looked up he was still standing there.

'Harry?'

'I had cancer, Annie. That's why I left. I know you don't want to hear this, but tough. A few weeks before we were due to go to Dubai, I got diagnosed. Testicular cancer. Aggressive. I didn't want you to wreck your life, give up on your dreams and nursemaid me instead. I was scared, Annie, and sick, and upset. I wasn't cheating on you or planning to. I didn't leave you, not like you thought. I loved you, Annie, so much. I just did what I thought was right. After your mum, I just couldn't put you through that again. It was bad, but my bosses in Dubai surprised me. They had a research centre over there, specialising in my illness. They offered to still take me, to keep my job on. I needed to earn, and I needed to get out of Dad's house. You know things were bad between us back then. I felt cornered, so I went. I just couldn't put you through that in a new country, all on your own. I got better, I got your call, and it gave me the hope I needed to come home, to try to win you back. And, as I keep saying, I'm back for good. Did you hear me, Annie? I didn't leave you because I wanted to, okay?'

She nodded, not trusting her voice to even make any coherent sound other than a strangled squeak. Everything he had just unloaded on her was swimming around in her head.

Cancer. He'd had cancer. He'd left her to spare her from going through it all again, and so he did it alone. He was just as alone as she was. More so. She felt her face redden as she played back in her head every time she'd nipped at him since he'd got back.

Harry spoke again, softer this time. He sounded so sad, but she couldn't get her head to lift to look at him. 'I'll go and get lunch, and when I get back we are going to talk about this.'

When the door closed and the sound of his footsteps disappeared, she stared at the wall, her grey matter trying to keep up with the flurry of information. *He was sick.* That was something she'd never considered on her list of reasons Harry had left. Not even once. Reaching for the phone in her pocket with paint-splattered fingers, she dialled Tom's number with shaky hands.

'Hey, girl! How's the painting coming along? We're just in the baby shop! I tell you, Lloyd is hammering the old plastic today! Will you tell him that a baby cosy toes is not essential for a pair of newborns? I swear, we need to do a Pinterest intervention at some point.'

Annabel broke down into racking sobs and when she tried to speak it came out as one big wail.

'Anna Banana, what's wrong? Lloyd, Annabel's upset, come here, quick.' She heard footsteps, the background noise of the busy shop die down, and then Tom and Lloyd's voices.

'You're on speakerphone, we're hiding in the disabled toilet. What's wrong?'

Where to start...?

'I kissed Harry! That's what's wrong! He showed up this morning with breakfast, and we were painting and...'

Lloyd, who was usually the calmer of the two, did a little whoop into the handset. 'Oh, wow, that's amazing! Why are you upset? I thought tha— Oof! Tom!'

She could hear the phone being wrestled from him, and Tom was the next to speak. 'Sorry about Mr Excited over here; he's been sniffing the baby talc. I have to say, though, I saw this coming.'

'What?' Annabel retorted crossly. 'I didn't. I didn't see any of this coming, and that's not all either. He had cancer, Tom. That's why he left. Not for some leggy blonde or because he didn't love me. Because he had cancer. He just told me, and then went out for sandwiches!' She sobbed again. Tom sighed, and she could hear him and Lloyd whispering to each other. 'Guys, help! I don't have long; he only went to get lunch. What the hell do I do? I've been awful to him since he got back, and he tried to tell me so many times. I'm evil, I didn't help him. I kept his son from him, I didn't listen to him. What the hell am I doing, Tom?'

The line was silent for what felt like forever.

'Tom?' she sniffed into the phone. 'You there? Please say you're there.'

'Sorry, it's just the shock. I'm processing. Poor Harry! I guess it makes sense, though, doesn't it? The Harry who left you wasn't the Harry we knew. I feel so bad now; I should have tried harder to reach him. He must have been really scared. I can't believe he just did that on his own. It must have been awful. But you kissed him though, right? So you didn't send him away after? Annabel, I've got to say, the writing was on the wall as soon as we saw him at the airport. You know the truth now; there's nothing holding you back, is there?'

'Yeah, and it's better than the writing on the wall in here. I mean, do they not teach spelling in school any more?' Lloyd's voice chipped in. Another muffled struggle, presumably Tom giving his husband another shove.

'Focus! What I mean is, well…you've hardly been happy since he left. I know you think you are, but you've never even looked at another man. We've tried to set you up with every straight man in a ten-mile radius, and you've never been bothered. Aidan's growing up now; what about you? Do you want to rattle around in that house like Miss Havisham in your retirement? I hated Harry for what he did, but he came back. He obviously went through something life-changing, but he still came back. I know it's crazy, but he obviously thought he was sparing you from going through what he faced. He knew your mum, what you both went through before you met us. He obviously never wanted to go. That means something, right?'

Annabel wiped her tears away with her free arm and nodded.

'Right?' Tom pressed.

'I'm nodding,' she retorted sulkily. 'He's only been back a short while though; why would he stay now? What's keeping him here, once the novelty fades? I can't go through that again. And then there's Aidan.'

'Exactly,' Lloyd spoke up. 'There is Aidan to think about. Don't you think he deserves a chance to be part of a family? We support all types of families, obviously, but you've done this alone for so long. It takes a village, right? Harry could be part of that village, honey.'

'He's Aidan's real father,' she blurted out. 'That changes everything.'

The line went quiet again, and Annabel held the phone away from her face to check that the call hadn't disconnected. 'Hello? You still there?'

'Give us a second. You keep dropping bombshells, and that's the first time you've admitted that to us.'

Now Annabel fell silent.

'Did she hang up? Call her back! Tom, call her back!' Lloyd's high-pitched tone made Annabel chuckle through her tears.

'I'm here. Nice return fire, by the way. Did you know Harry was Aidan's father the whole time?'

'Er…well…' Tom floundered.

'Yes, we did. Don't forget, we know you. The timing made sense, and we scraped you off your bedroom floor when he left. There's no way that you'd have entertained another man. Then or now. We took you out, remember? There was no man. Aside from the ones you brushed off, and the one you threatened to throat punch for getting handsy.'

Annabel cried again, half laughing, half wailing.

They'd never questioned her or judged her once. She loved them all the more for it.

'I wish you'd said something.'

'You never said anything either; you shut us down whenever we got near to asking. We figured you would in time, but you never did. We wanted to respect your wishes. We get it, Annabel. We already hated Harry.'

'Yeah, I feel sorry for that now; we need to send him a fruit basket or something.'

'Lloyd, shush! Has Harry met Aidan yet?' Tom asked.

'He's living with Abe, so yeah. Aidan doesn't know though.' A thought occurred to her and she felt as if ice water had been poured down her back. 'Does that mean everyone knows? Oh, no, I can't do this. He's working at the station—what am I going to do? I have to end this, now. There's too much at stake. I can't risk Aidan getting hurt; he's had such a tough time lately.'

She could hear footsteps on the path once more, and the whistle that Harry used to do, the one he always did when he was happy. He thought that there was a chance now. Maybe he was just feeling lighter now he'd spoken his truth. She'd done that. She'd messed up, muddied the waters. She needed to undo it.

'He's coming, I've got to go.'

'Wait, Annabel! Don't do what I think you're going to do. Stop being so scared! He told you why he left! This is what you want! Stop hiding!'

She ripped open the last of the packages at speed, her phone shoved between her chin and her shoulder. She didn't want him to think she'd been sitting there blubbing since he'd left, even though she had.

'I can't do it, Tom, it's too late. It's too complicated! I'll call you later, okay?' She ended the call, Lloyd and Tom's protestations ringing in her ears as she shoved the phone back into her back pocket. When Harry walked in a second later, a carrier bag swinging from one arm, she was sitting cross-legged, her face hidden by her hair as she stacked up the assortment of bits she'd bought for the house, and for Aidan.

'Hey,' he said, shutting the door and coming to sit beside her. 'I got some doughnuts too, and extra for Aidan after school.' His smile crumpled when she turned to look at him. 'Oh, God, I'm sorry. I shouldn't have just dropped all that on you and left. Are you okay?'

Annabel pushed the items to one side, and she reached for the sandwich he was proffering in his hand.

'I'm okay; it was just a shock.'

'Not like me, dropping bad news and running off. I'm glad you know, though. I've wanted to tell you forever. And the kiss was amazing. Just like before. Better even.'

She reached for his arm, pulling him down to sit next to her. 'Harry, that kiss was—'

'One of the three greatest things that has happened to me in the last year. The first being when you called me, and the second finding out you'd had our son.'

He gripped her hand in his and she pulled it away, putting her hands on the top of her knees to stop them doing their own thing and reaching for him. He looked at his empty hand, and then the floor.

'You still don't trust me, do you?'

'Why didn't you just tell me about the cancer? How bad was it? What treatment did you have?'

'It was bad enough. Stage two. I had three tumours, I had to have some lymph nodes removed. Intensive treatment. I was a cue ball up top for a while.' He swallowed hard, pushing his food away. 'I didn't tell you because you would have come with me. You'd have travelled to a different country and put your life on hold, and I didn't want that for you. I was terrified, Annie, and I couldn't put you through that. Not after all that you went through with your mum. I was there for that; I saw how bad it was.'

Annabel thought of her mother, the pain she'd gone through. She would have been by his side in a heartbeat.

'I would have liked to have been given the choice. You took that decision out of my hands. You made me feel like dirt, embarrassed me in front of everyone. I would have helped you, been there. What if you had died, Harry? How do you think that would have gone? How everyone back here would have taken that news?'

Harry came to her, and his hands were cupping her face. He touched his forehead to hers. 'I know. I was stupid,' he whispered. 'I've regretted it every day since I left, but at the time I was so sick and scared, I just thought it was the right thing. Then, after, I...'

'All that time though.' She shook her head, pulling away a little to look into his eyes. 'You pushed everyone away. How did you even cope, out there on your own? Why didn't you answer us when we called?' Her voice tapered off into a choked sob. 'You must have been so scared, so lonely. I can't bear it, Harry. What on earth were you thinking?' Once again, she was flip-flopping from feeling awful for him and wanting to slap him for being such a stubborn fool. He could have had everyone around him, and he could have had his son. She would have looked after them both; she knew she would. Just thinking about it made her upset all over again. She didn't like feeling out of control, and he hadn't even trusted her when she'd needed him most.

'I can't believe you didn't even tell anyone. You went through that all on your own, but you had me, Harry. You had me! You had all of us! I can't understand the lie you told us all.'

'I wasn't thinking straight. I was fresh out of training, young and terrified. I wasn't going to see the next year out. What about your lie?' he countered, sitting back on his haunches, away from her. 'You never told anyone about Aidan, not the truth. I'm his father. What about what you took from me? Don't you think I deserved to know? You stopped calling a couple of months after I left. No one told me about him, Annie, not even my own father. I missed out on my son's whole life because of you, and I didn't deserve that.'

Annabel reeled back. She'd been expecting this in the back of her mind, but it still felt like a slap in the face.

'You left me—what was I supposed to do? I didn't know you were sick, did I?'

'Oh, I don't know. Write me a letter, pick up the phone. Send me a sonogram, maybe! Anything would have been better. What if I'd never come back? You called me months ago to tell me to come home, and you knew what I'd be walking into.'

'Oh, yeah, that would have been a great phone call: *Harry, I hate you, but you left me a baby when you went.* How would you have taken that, mid treatment?'

'Forget about the treatment! Did you not think I had a right to know? I'm not the only one who lied here.' His eyes were shining with anger, and Annabel didn't have a retort.

He lied, I lied. So much wasted time. We can never come back from this. Anything I've been fantasising about just seems too hard now.

'I know. I have no room to talk. I have my own regrets, even more now I know the truth, but it's too late now. I wanted to protect myself, and Aidan. I nearly called, so many times.'

'Yeah? Well, I wish you had,' he spat back, his anger still evidently controlling him. 'I never got a choice in that decision either.'

He was so cold. It sent her barriers clanging right back up around her.

'Yeah, well, we can hash this out all day, can't we, but it just proves my point. We shouldn't be together, Harry. There's enough water under our bridge to sink the whole thing.'

Harry's jaw flexed, and she looked away. She realised she'd been hoping for him to fight, deep down, but there were two deeply hurt people in the room now. He'd lied to her; she'd lied right back. Not exactly the basis for a loving relationship.

'We have Aidan to think about. Whatever this is, he has to be the priority.'

'I agree,' Harry said, his voice thick with sadness. 'That's it then. So no more kissing, right?'

'Right,' she agreed. 'I'm sorry, Harry. I really am. Are you well now? I know it's a bit late to ask now, but what happened? What was the prognosis?'

It took him a minute, and then he was opening his sandwich.

'I don't really want to talk about it right now. I'm fine, healthy as a horse. You know now; that's the main thing. We'd better get back to work. I don't want to fight any more.' He was looking straight at her, but all she could see on his face was disappointment. She could identify the emotion because she was pretty sure it was etched across her features. Tom and Lloyd were going to kill her. 'Let's get these eaten; we have a lot to do before school's out.'

She sneaked a few glances at him as they ate in the quiet of the house, but he didn't look her way again, and then they were back to work.

Harry was in the kitchen washing his hands free of grey paint when he heard hurried little footsteps heading towards the house. He looked across at Annabel, who was busy tidying away.

'Should I go?' he checked. They'd worked quietly for the rest of the day, apart from a few awkward 'Pass me the roller, please' or 'Another tea?'. He'd finally been able to tell her everything, but it had gone far from the way he'd wanted it to. They still weren't together, and the recriminations were thicker than the paint fumes in the room. It was a start, at least, but the afternoon had gone a little differently to the morning. The dancing, the kiss, the heat between them. The radio had been on low, but this time no one danced.

'No, it's fine,' she managed to reply before their son barrelled through the door. She gave him a little smile, and he flashed her one back. He was mad at her but he still loved her, more than ever. He wished he could go back and shake their younger selves, make them talk to each other.

'Mum, Mum! Guess what!'

She smiled at Harry, her face lighting up properly for the first time since lunch. 'I hope you're ready for this; he's a chatterbox after school.' She headed out to meet Aidan, and he met her in the kitchen doorway.

'We get to take someone to school for career day! I can't wait! Toby's dad is a pig farmer, and he's going to bring in a piglet!'

'Oh, really? That's so cool!' Harry said to him, and Aidan turned and noticed him for the first time. 'Your mother used to love piglets back when we were kids.'

He saw Annabel go rigid, and he replayed the words in his head.

'You knew my mum when she was little. I forgot!' Aidan exclaimed, all thoughts of the piglet forgotten as he looked from one adult to the other. 'What was she like? Granddad always says she was born with ants in her pants.'

Annabel laughed, leaning across to ruffle his hair.

He brushed her hand off, smoothing it back down with a mini scowl on his mini-me face. 'Mum! Don't mess up my hair!'

This had Harry and Annabel both laughing. Harry knelt down, closer to Aidan's eye level. 'Mums do that, kiddo, and your mum was a little tornado when she was younger.' His gaze flicked to hers. 'She still is. Who are you taking to career day?'

Aidan gave his mum a sidelong look and moved a bit closer. 'Well, I was going to take Mum, but I don't know after today. Jade said her mum's an air stewardess, and she gets to go on aeroplanes for free. I was going to ask Granddad, but he's pretty old now.'

'Aidan!' Annabel chided softly. 'Abe isn't that old.'

Aidan rolled his eyes theatrically. 'He likes old things though, and Jamal's mum is a doctor too, so that would be super boring.'

'GPs *are* super boring,' Harry agreed, laughing. His heart was racing just being near his son. He wanted to scoop him up, give him a hug, but he was all too aware that Annabel was watching the pair of them as if she was waiting for a bomb to go off. He had a thought then. It was a risk, but one he was willing to take. A shot at one of the final lies that stood between them all, the elephant in the room. 'You know, I've been on a few aeroplanes myself, for work. How about me and your mum come together? Would that be better?'

Annabel's sharp gasp went unnoticed by Aidan, but Harry heard it loud and clear.

'If the station would let us have the time off, of course.' He glanced at her now, trying his best to gauge her mood. She looked like a rabbit caught in the headlights. Aidan was bouncing on the spot between them.

'Really? Oh, Mum, that would be so cool. Can you both come?' He made a batting motion with his hands. 'That would knock the other kids out of the park!' He bounced over to his mother and pulled at her hands excitedly. 'Mum, come on, *please*!'

'Well, I'm sure that Harry has other things to do than come to your school, honey.'

'I really haven't,' Harry countered, pushing his luck now but still desperate to prove himself to them both. The thought of having an insight into Aidan's school life, his friends, and the world he inhabited was so appealing it was worth risking Annabel's wrath. He didn't enjoy her discomfort, but she had called him. She'd told him about Aidan and, despite their failed kiss and their fight, he still felt that the embers of hope had been stoked. He couldn't just shut his feelings off, even if he wanted to. He wanted to drain the water from under their bridge.

'If it's okay with the boss, I would love to come.'

Aidan's face lit up. 'Yes! Mum, can I go online now? I want to tell Finn and Josh!' He was already heading up the stairs at this point, and Annabel let him go.

'Just until your tea's ready, okay?'

'Yeah! Okay!' he shouted down the stairs, before his door slammed shut. Not long after, they could hear the *pew-pew* of the game and Aidan laughing and chatting excitedly with his friends.

'He loves that game,' Annabel said, walking past Harry to start tea. 'I've tried to play it loads of times, but I always die before I manage to land.'

Opening the freezer door, she took a second to gather her thoughts without Harry's gaze on her. The cold air helped to cool her face, which felt as if it was on fire. First today, and now this. She would be going into school with him, while every kid in the class hung on his word and stories of faraway adventures. She wanted to know about his life, so it would be good to hear, but all she could think about was the fact that she'd been left behind, and why. When she'd thought he was jet-setting and making his mark, she was raising a child, keeping his secret, and he was facing his own battle on his own.

She couldn't bear it. She hated the bitterness and bubbling fear that rose within her at inconvenient times; it kept her away from Harry as much as she wanted to let him in. The barb he had thrown at her regarding Aidan still smarted. He was right, but it was one more thing that they had between them. They could have the chance of being the family she'd always secretly wanted, and now she felt wretched at the thought of it never happening. She hated herself for being so weak, so wishy-washy in her decision-making, and her mother would have gone mad. She was almost glad that she wasn't here to see any of it. She'd died confident in the knowledge that her only child had Harry by her side.

* * *

'Listen, it's been a long day,' Harry said from behind her, and she knew he was close. 'Don't bother cooking for you and Aidan; I could get us a pizza or something, or we could go out to eat? I was hoping we could talk more. I need to clear the air.'

Grabbing a couple of steamed vegetable bags from the icy depths, she turned to him.

'We have a rule, no junk food in the week. I'm grateful for your help today, but I do need to crack on with getting things sorted. Once Aidan's in bed, I'm planning to crash myself. We have homework, the usual stuff to get through. I'll see you at work tomorrow.' She tried to be as sweet as possible, but she could tell by his face that he was disappointed. 'I have to keep things normal around here. Aidan's had a lot to deal with lately. I'll see you at the station, okay? It's been a bit of a revelation day; I'm having trouble processing things.'

Harry looked at her for a long moment, and slowly nodded. 'I overstepped.'

'You overstepped,' she echoed. 'Honestly,

Harry, it's just a lot. I am trying. I'm sorry I never told you about him. I really am. I'm sorry for a lot of things.'

'I get it, Annie. I don't really have room to talk, do I?'

'I guess not, but I get it now. See you at work? I promise a ceasefire.'

He held his hands up in surrender, before tiptoeing forward on the lightest of feet and bending his head to hers. 'Me too,' he said softly, dropping the tiniest brush of his lips against her cheek and, before she could blink, he was heading to the hallway and out of the door.

She looked at the thawing bags of vegetables on the countertop and touched her hand to the spot where Harry's lips had touched her skin. Turning on the radio, she poured herself a glass of wine before attempting to turn her attention back to the daily chores. The lines between her real life and the life she'd always pictured were blurring, and it was getting harder and harder to see which one was the real one. Or which one she really wanted.

CHAPTER FIVE

HARRY WALKED INTO the station bright and early, eager to get the day going now he was finally getting settled back into work. Over the last few weeks he'd been spending time with Aidan and his dad, reconnecting with his father slowly and getting to know the amazing little boy who still didn't know he was his father.

Annabel had kept him at arm's length since the day at the house, and although she didn't flinch as much when he was around her any more, she wasn't letting her guard down either. There were no more barbed comments, but the atmosphere between them was still charged. They'd not spoken about their fight, neither seeming to want to rock the boat.

He caught her watching him sometimes, at work, when he was playing with Aidan or talking shop with his dad. They were together a lot, and she never stopped watching him. Sometimes, he wanted to ask her what she was thinking, what the frowns and worried expressions meant, but he was still scared of spooking her again. When he did finally ask her the question that burned deep in his heart, he wanted to be sure of the answer. Anything less would kill him.

He'd waited a long time to be back in her life, and now that he was back, and had a real chance, he didn't want to risk blowing it again. Too much was at stake for all of them. They'd both kept secrets from each other, but now they were out there he saw a real chance for them, the three of them, if they could get over their past.

The school career day was coming up at the end of the month, and Aidan was still so excited about them both coming to present to his class; he'd spoken of nothing else. She hadn't stopped that, so he found himself wondering what his next move should be as he wandered into the staffroom to get a much-needed cup of coffee. The stuff Abe bought tasted like the bottom of a birdcage.

The moment he walked in he immediately regretted his caffeine addiction. It was full of people, and he was still tiptoeing around some of them. He decided to get what he needed and get out of there. Saying 'Hello' as he walked in, the room growing quieter in his presence, he filled his cup from the coffeemaker, taking a deep gulp of the hot black liquid before turning back to the door.

He bumped into Annabel, who was just coming into the room. 'Turn back around,' he said, taking her under the elbow and steering her away.

'What?' Annabel craned her neck over his shoulder. 'But I need coffee!'

He handed her his cup, walking them both to the room where they carried out the handovers.

'There you go. It's a full house in there.'

'Ugh.' She pulled a face and Harry sniggered. 'I wanted breakfast though!'

'I'll buy you a bacon roll when we hit the road. Why didn't you eat before you left?'

She rolled her eyes at him. 'That would be something. I'm all about getting Aidan up and out on a morning. I swear he's hitting his teens early.' She took the cup in both hands and took a drink as though she'd just emerged from the desert. 'Ahh, hello, my delicious dark lord.'

Harry laughed, and she elbowed him playfully.

'Knock it off, I'm having a moment here.'

'Oh, I know not to bother you before coffee.' They nodded to a couple of passing nurses as they neared their destination.

'You remember that, eh?' she teased, taking another sip.

'I remember everything. Every little detail,' he said, waggling his eyebrows. She blushed, and his heart skipped a beat. 'Come on and bring the dark lord. Let's get this show on the road. I can already smell the bacon.'

In the last few weeks they'd fallen into a sort of uneasy groove with each other. The tension at work had lessened, although she'd never quite managed to quell the butterflies that still fluttered in the pit of her stomach when Harry leaned in close in the ambulance, or when they witnessed a tender moment with one of their patients. She'd even cried on him when one of the calls had been a bad one, and he'd held her and let her sob her heart out on him without even a second's hesitation. Feeling his arms around her had made her feel so supported, and she knew he a hundred per cent had her back. Just as he had before. He was every bit the paramedic she was, and they had soon dropped back into their old shorthand way of communicating and working on the job. As she went to reach for something, he was already in the process of passing it to her, and vice versa. It made them the ultimate team, and the station had started to hum with the buzz of them being back together.

With the career day coming up, she no longer dreaded it as she had. In fact, she was rather looking forward to it. Not that she'd tell him that. She'd found herself watching him with their son, and when they were on the job together. She was imagining what he'd gone through with his cancer, worrying about how he had come through it. How he felt now. He and Abe were even different together. They laughed now, the recriminations of the past seemingly starting to resolve. She was so glad; she knew that Abe had been so upset about his son's disappearance. Having Aidan around him had helped, but it would never replace his son. She understood that because no one would ever take the place of Aidan in her own heart.

By watching Harry—her Harry—she knew without a shadow of a doubt that he was in there too, right next to Aidan in the beating organ in her chest, and she knew that really he had never left. Now all she needed to do was decide whether she followed the beat of her heart or her head. Her mind was flip-flopping on a daily basis, and she didn't quite know which one to trust. So she stayed in limbo. Looking for a sign, a concrete reason? She just didn't know. So she focused on what she did know. The daily grind, her job, her son. Everything else was just too confusing to see clearly.

With the handover done, the two of them were soon on their way, a princely breakfast fuelling their busy day. And a busy day it turned out to be. Two calls for chest pains, four elderly falls, one woman going into labour at home alone, and more than a dozen slips, scrapes and work-related injuries.

'Wow, London is just full of poorly people today.' Harry arched his back, shifting in the passenger seat of ambulance seventeen.

Annabel drove through the city streets, focused on the traffic but flashing him a tired smile. 'I know, and not one camel in sight.'

'Ha-ha.' Harry stuck his tongue out at her. 'Funny. It's not all desert dust and camels, you know.'

The next call came in, and Harry took care of the details while Annabel put the lights and sirens on, following the quickest route to the casualty while Harry fed back their ETA to the control room.

'Eight-year-old child, male, difficulty breathing. Mother is very anxious. High temp overnight first controlled with paracetamol and ibuprofen, but now the fever is spiking and he is unable to speak more than a few words without difficulty. Query for a possible asthma attack.'

Annabel's lips pursed, and once the road opened up she put her foot down on the accelerator. They pulled up outside the house in no time and were greeted by a man standing at the garden gate. He had a cigarette in one hand and a can of strong lager in the other. Harry nodded at the man, and his eyes focused on Annabel's.

'You get the equipment; I'll go in first.' Annabel rolled her eyes at him, but something about the man made her follow his lead for once. Their priority was the little boy inside. Harry got out and approached the gate.

'Hello, sir—you called for assistance?'

Annabel worked quickly, Harry talking to the man, who was swaying and bumping into the gate.

'I didn't. Her indoors did. I told her, Ben's just trying it on. Coughing and wheezing all night. Kept us all up. He just doesn't want to go to school. You're wasting your time, mate, and your little woman here. Last thing I want is another panic-stricken female in the place.'

'Well, we're here now. Is Ben your son?' He didn't like the way the man was sneering at Annabel. He obviously had little respect for women.

'Stepson,' the man countered, not even looking at Annabel as she came to stand at the side of Harry. Neither of them missed the sneer on his face as he spoke. The man pointed a thumb behind him towards the house, showering ash from his cigarette over himself. 'She panders to him too much; it's only a cold.'

'Can we come past, please?' Harry said, his hand already on the gate. The man slowly and sluggishly moved aside, and Harry caught hold of Annabel's shirt sleeve, taking one of the kit bags from her and leading her into the property.

'Hello?' Annabel called into the hallway.

'Up here,' a panicked female voice said. 'Quickly, please! Second bedroom on the left.'

The house was neat and tidy, aside from a

full ashtray and a few empty cans littering the coffee table. A sports channel was on in the background, and they could hear the weak murmurs of the boy as they ran up the stairs.

'I told you, you're wasting your time. Isn't there anyone else you could be helping? I've warned her not to push my buttons.' The man was shouting up the stairs now, but the paramedics were already focused on the boy laid on the top of a single bed, his mother looking hollow-eyed and utterly panicked.

'Hi, Ben,' Annabel said, walking into the room as slowly as she could without losing time or panicking the boy. 'We're here to help, okay?'

The little boy was red-faced and because he was bare-chested, wearing only character pyjama bottoms, she could tell from his torso that he was really struggling to breathe. The little mite nodded, and the pair of them got to work. They listened to his chest, put a monitor on his finger and took his blood pressure.

'Mum, is it?' Harry said softly, turning to the woman while Annabel hooked Ben up to the portable oxygen tank they had carried in.

'Julie, yeah. Is he going to be okay?'

'We're here to get him sorted; this oxygen will help him breathe better, get his stats back up,' he said smoothly. 'Has he had any difficulties like this before? Any asthma, or any history in the family?'

The worried mother shook her head, never taking her eyes off the boy. 'No, nothing like that. I don't think the smoke's been helping him though.' She looked at the doorway now, wide-eyed, as if her partner was standing there, but when Annabel looked, it was empty. The television channel had been changed downstairs, the noise blaring out. 'He started with a cold a couple of days ago. Nothing major, but after last night I just couldn't keep his temperature down for long, and now...'

She crumpled, dropping a kiss on her son's head and keeping him close.

'Oxygen's low, decreased breath sounds on both sides,' Annabel said quietly, and Harry nodded once.

'Julie, we need to pop Ben up to the hospital, get him checked over properly. Can you grab him what he needs, and we'll set off? It sounds like he's got a nasty chest infection. I'll go get a chair. Be ready to transport.'

He didn't want to be carrying Ben down the stairs, and he had a feeling that the man downstairs wouldn't be very pleased with the idea that the emergency services were 'entertaining' his stepson and his illness. He walked out of the room, running to the ambulance as soon as the boy was out of sight, heading upstairs with the chair as quickly and nimbly as he could.

'Hey!' The man got up from the couch as Harry got halfway up the stairs. 'What the hell are you doing? Woman, I warned you!'

Harry ignored him, entering the boy's room and closing the door behind him. He didn't hear anything further, but the television volume went up again. Harry clenched his jaw and focused on the job in hand. He wanted to get the boy out of this place, and the fact that Annabel was here was making him nervous. The urge to protect her was raging through his body. He couldn't bear the thought of her being hurt. Someone with a temper and a drink in them was not a good combination.

Not on my watch, he thought, and they got the boy out of there as fast as they could.

Much later, after Ben was settled in the care of the staff at A&E, Annabel followed Harry out to the ambulance.

'Well, I thought that might go south at one point. I thought we might need to call for police assistance. He was a piece of work, wasn't he? I felt sorry for them both.'

Harry didn't reply, and when they'd got back into the ambulance she looked at him with concern.

'You need a minute? We have a little time, if you need it.'

'I'll never understand people like that. The poor boy was ill; she'd have called before if it wasn't for him, I'm sure. He could have got so much worse.'

'He didn't though; he's going to be fine. We got to him, got him help.'

Harry responded through gritted teeth.

'That's not the point, and you know it. The kid deserved a father to be there for him.'

'You don't know that he hasn't. Families split up; it doesn't always mean that the father isn't on the scene, or that he doesn't care.'

'I hate that Aidan never had that.' He looked away from her, gazing out at the hospital's comings and goings. 'I hate that he thinks his father isn't in his life.'

'It's not like that, and at the time I—'

'I'm not having a go; it's just hard, that's all. I don't blame you. I get your reasons. I hate them, but I get it. The thought of you getting hurt today… It tore me apart. I would have taken that guy's head off if he'd come near you.'

'You don't have to worry. I can look after myself.'

'That's not what I'm saying. I know you can, but I want to be the one who looks after you too.'

He grabbed for her hand, taking it into his and placing it in his lap.

'I don't blame you; I blame myself. For everything.'

Not knowing what to say, how to make it right, Annabel squeezed his hand and then pulled away, clicking on the console that they were available for another call.

'We've got another hour; let's shake that last call off.'

He didn't reply, pulling on his seatbelt and jamming it violently into the holder.

She looked at him thoughtfully. 'Listen, it's Friday, and it's been a week. You got plans for tonight?'

That turned his head in her direction. She gave him a little smile.

'I think Dad has his poker buddies coming round. I was just planning to stay out of the way. Sleep off the day.'

'Well, as good as *that* sounds, I was thinking I might have a night off from cooking and order Chinese food with Aidan, maybe watch a film.' He looked bemused, and she patted his hand. 'I was thinking you could come over, share some noodles?'

He still looked drawn, but the lines on his

brow lessened as he gave her a grateful smile. 'Noodles and a movie sound great. What time?'

Annabel, fresh from the shower, listened to Aidan giggle downstairs as he watched one of his favourite TV shows, camped on the couch under his comfy throw. The canned laughter from the comedy show filtered upstairs, and she smiled to herself as she thought of her son, sitting in his pyjamas, waiting for Harry to arrive. He'd be here soon, and the minute they'd left each other in the hospital car park, the butterflies had started. She was looking forward to it so much, and Aidan's face when she'd told him had made her heart sing.

They did rattle around a bit in the new house. When he was in bed fast asleep, she ended up going to bed early half the time, bored of sitting alone and looking at the newly decorated walls or the list of stuff she still wanted to get done. Tonight would be a welcome change, and she couldn't help but think of it as a trial run either. Which meant she found herself wanting to make the effort, just a little.

She turned to her wardrobe and the half dozen outfits she had picked out as possibilities for the evening. They verged from ballroom attire to full-on sex kitten, and she groaned at her choices.

'Get a grip on yourself,' she chided her reflection in the mirror. She put them all back into the wardrobe and, heading to her dresser drawer, she pulled out her comfy black jeans and a white T-shirt. There. Not too much, but she did look good. She made to head downstairs, but at the last minute she blow-dried her hair so it fell in waves around her face, and slicked on a little bit of pink lip gloss. 'There, nothing too much.'

She nodded at herself in the bedroom mirror and headed downstairs just in time to hear the knock at the door. She took a second to quell the frisson of nerves that fizzed through her body and, taking a deep breath, she stepped into the hall.

'Hi.' She opened the door to Harry, who looked stunning in a blue checked shirt, open at the neck, paired with dark blue jeans. She wanted to laugh as she took him in but held it back. They had both tried a little too hard to look casual, it seemed. 'Come in.'

'Hi.' Harry smiled, stepping into the hallway and looking around him. 'Wow, the builders really cracked on with the place. It's looking great.'

'Thanks. I'm still picking dust bunnies up but yeah, it's getting there now.'

Annabel motioned him to come into the kitchen, and she noticed for the first time that he was bearing gifts. One was a football, and the other a beautiful bunch of flowers. She'd been so focused on him, she'd never even registered what was in his arms. The lounge in the TV was still playing, and Aidan's laughter filtered through to them. He hadn't heard the door.

'Selective hearing,' she explained. 'His show finishes soon. Come through?'

Harry eyed the doorway to the lounge but followed her through with a nod. 'I brought you some housewarming gifts. Thanks for inviting me tonight; it's already getting rowdy at home.'

Annabel's heart warmed when she heard that he considered Abe's to be home. The pair of them were so similar, they'd always butted heads. Abe had seemingly let go of the GP father-son dream, and when Annabel saw the two of them these days they seemed to be rubbing along quite nicely together, rowdy card nights aside. It made her so happy, after all those years of them being at loggerheads. It was nice to see, and Abe was far happier and less grumpy to boot. Win-win. He hadn't even been angry at her for keeping the truth about Aidan a secret, which had surprised her too. Given their struggles over the years, it could have been a heck of a lot worse. Of course, Abe had kept his own counsel for years. He'd never let Annabel know that he'd worked it out. Like she'd said, they were so similar in many ways.

'No problem. Aidan's been looking forward to it. If he wasn't glued to his programme, he'd already be in here chewing your ear off.' She took the flowers from him, leaning in to smell the blooms. 'Calla lilies too, my favourite.' Her hair fell over her eye and Harry leaned in, brushing the strand away with his free hand.

'I know. I remember.' She shivered when his fingertips brushed down her cheek and, closing her eyes, she turned her face into his hand. His eyes went dark and he leaned in, just a fraction. The paper wrapping the flowers being squashed between them rustled as she followed his lead.

'Is that for me?'

Aidan bounded into the room, and the pair of them sprang apart. Harry threw her a look that made her pulse race and addressed his enthusiastic son.

'Of course it is! I thought, with your new garden being sorted, you could get some practice in.'

Harry whirled around on the balls of his feet, leaning down to show Aidan the football. Annabel knew it was a decent one; Harry had been eyeing it in the shop the other week when they'd been shopping for new boots.

'It's so cool! Thanks, Harry! Look, Mum!'

Aidan took the ball from Harry's hands, showing her his gift.

'Oh, that's great! We'll have to get a football net for out back; you can show us some skills.'

Aidan's expression was so happy and, looking at Harry's flushed face, she could tell he was equally elated. His red cheeks also gave him away as feeling just as caught out by their son as she did. The two of them started to chat away, and she busied herself by finding a vase for the flowers. They really were beautiful. She couldn't remember the last time a man had bought her any. Harry had always been a romantic in the past.

This is a housewarming gift, though, not a declaration.

Even her own thoughts sounded unsure. If they hadn't been interrupted, she'd have kissed him again. Glancing back at Harry, who was looking at her over Aidan's shoulder, she felt certain that he knew it too.

'Another prawn toast?'

Aidan shook his head, groaning as he patted his little flat tummy. 'No, thanks, Mum, I'm stuffed!'

Harry sat back next to him on the couch, patting his own belly. 'Nor me, I can't do it.'

The feast was sitting out on the coffee table, the credits of the family film they had just finished watching rolling on screen.

'Well, more for me then. Waste not, want not!'

Annabel swooped in for the last piece, eating it in two bites.

Harry chuckled, a low rumble. 'You always were like a dustbin,' he teased.

'Hey!' She flicked out a foot from her sideways position on the armchair, trying to kick him. He didn't flinch, just grabbed her bare foot. His touch made her skin tingle, and he stroked the top of her foot and slowly let it go.

Aidan was giggling at the side of him 'He's right Mum; you always order too much and then eat your way through it.' He made a snorting pig sound, and Harry joined in. She pretended to glare at them both, and caught Aidan stifling a yawn.

'Well, piglet, I think that means it's time for you to go to bed.'

'Aww, no!' he tried to protest, but another yawn cut him off. 'Okay,' he said glumly. ''Night, Harry.' He flung himself into Harry's chest, hugging him tight.

Harry looked shocked for a half second, before wrapping his arms around him and kissing the top of his head. ''Night, kiddo, sleep tight. And hey, if you want a goalie, I'm in.'

'Cool. Can we, Mum?' He lifted his head to look at his mother, and she found herself a little too choked to speak, seeing the two of them cuddled up on the couch, so natural with each other. She nodded and smiled robotically, pointing a finger towards the hallway.

'I know, I know—brush my teeth. 'Night, Harry!' He held out a hand and Harry high-fived him back.

''Night, Aidan. Sleep tight.'

'I won't be long. Make yourself at home,' she said over her shoulder as she headed up the stairs after her son.

Once teeth were brushed and hands and

face were washed, Aidan snuggled down under the covers. Annabel tucked him in, turning his dinosaur night light down to low so the room glowed with a dull hue. The light from the landing trickled in, showing Aidan's tired face over the covers.

'Harry's so cool, Mum. He played football when he worked away, you know. I want to do that when I grow up.'

'Did he?'

'Yeah, he played with the other doctors. You should start a team, Mum, at the ambulance station. Harry could be the striker.'

Annabel laughed, sitting down on the bed and smoothing a tuft of hair off his face. 'Well, I think the nurses might like that, but there's no way I'd be getting my lily-white legs out in front of my colleagues and showing them how rubbish at the game I am.'

Another giggle filled the room. 'Yeah, you're rubbish.'

'Hey! I was great at netball at school, I'll have you know.'

That just produced an eye roll of epic proportions.

'That's lame, Mum. Messi is way cooler than any netball player.'

'I'll give you that,' she said, dropping a kiss on the top of her beautiful son's head. Seeing Harry and Aidan together had made her realise just how alike they were in their mannerisms. The eye rolls, the mickey taking. Harry always had been cheeky, and Aidan was just the same. She wondered what else she had blocked out about the past. 'Straight to sleep now.'

He turned onto his side, facing Annabel and resting his head on the plump pillows beneath him.

Sleepily, his eyelids already hooded, his brow furrowed. 'I like Harry. Do you, Mum?'

'Yes, I like him. He's good to work with.'

'I think he likes you too.'

'What makes you say that?'

'He looks at you a lot. Like how Uncle Tom and Uncle Lloyd look at each other.'

'Well, your uncles are in love, so it's a bit different.'

'I think it's the same. I think he likes you, Mum. Do you like him?'

'Of course I like him. He's a good friend, and we work together a lot so that's a good thing.'

'That's not what I meant, Mum.'

Annabel smiled down at him, fighting to stay awake as his busy day started to take its toll.

'I know, love. It's grown-up stuff; sometimes it's a bit complicated.'

'I know,' he said, showing wisdom far beyond his years. 'I just think that people who love each other should always say it. That's what Granddad says, and he's really smart.'

Annabel said nothing, her throat not co-operating now. She played with his fringe, just like she'd done when he was little, dropping another kiss onto his little forehead and watching in silence as his long dark lashes fluttered as he fell asleep. She was halfway out of his bedroom door when his soft voice, thick with sleep, stilled her departure.

'Do you think he'll stay forever? I really hope he does. We need him now, don't we?'

She turned to ask him what he meant, but he was already fast asleep.

'Yes, kiddo,' she whispered into the half light of the room. 'I think we do.'

Heading downstairs, she walked into the lounge and saw it was empty. The coffee table had been cleared, the cushions plumped and the television turned off. Just as her heart was sinking at the thought that Harry had left, she heard humming coming from the kitchen.

'You didn't have to do that,' she said from the doorway, watching him wash up at the sink. He looked so at home in her kitchen, as though he had always been there. Here in this house, with her.

'I don't mind, the least I could do really. I had a great night.' He turned to look at her as he placed another clean plate onto the dish rack. 'Aidan asleep already?'

'Yeah,' she said, crossing the room and taking a bottle of white wine from the fridge. 'He was exhausted.' The leftovers from their meal had been wrapped up and put into the fridge. 'You even saved me some snacks!'

He laughed, another low rumble. 'I couldn't find a trough, so I improvised.' He dried his hands on one of the towels from the rack and leaned back against the sink, his forearms flexing under his rolled-up shirtsleeves.

'Carry on with the sow jokes, I dare you.' She waggled the wine bottle at him. 'Drink?'

'Sure. Dad send a text a few minutes ago, complaining that Leonard is cheating. He mentioned something about 1976, so I'm guessing it's not the first time they've butted heads. I'm in no hurry. Glasses?'

'Behind you, top cabinet.'

They took them through to the lounge, sitting next to each other on the couch. Annabel flicked on the television, some comedy sitcom on low.

'You feeling better, after the Ben call?' She'd wanted to ask him since the minute he'd walked in but hadn't wanted to spoil the mood.

'Not really, but I checked with A&E. He's in for the night for observation. Mum's staying with him.'

Annabel filled both their glasses, offering one to Harry. Their hands crossed on the stem, and he stroked his finger along hers before taking it.

'That's good. I checked with the social care team. They are in the system, so I flagged up today's call with them. They'll check in with mum before they leave the hospital.'

Harry's shoulders relaxed a little, and he took a deep gulp of the cold drink. 'Thanks. I had been thinking the same thing, to be honest.'

'No problem. I would have done it anyway; the family needs some help. The mother's always worked well with them, by all accounts.'

Harry nodded. 'I got that feel from her. She obviously loves him.'

They fell silent, watching the television for a while in comfortable silence.

'I'd rather die than see Aidan suffer like that,' he said eventually, turning towards her on the couch. She tucked her feet up behind her, their knees touching now.

'I know that. He thinks you're amazing.'

'As a friend of his mum's, sure,' he retorted, his jaw flexing. 'As some long-lost son of his granddad.'

This isn't going how I thought it would. He's...angry.

'I don't want to argue, please. We're doing okay, aren't we?'

Harry sighed, and the anger seemed to leave his features. 'Sure. I've loved getting to know him. Dad's been great too. It's weird—the old issues, they just don't seem to be an issue any more.'

'He missed you, a lot. He did try to contact you; they all did.'

'I know,' he acknowledged. 'I just wasn't in the right frame of mind to hear from them.' He looked her right in the eye. 'I would have answered when you called again. I was on shift. I wish I'd called.'

She was mid sip, the rim of the glass resting on her lips. She finished the action, allowing the wine to cool her throat and give her strength. She'd almost bitten down on the glass when he'd spoken, but she had nowhere to hide with him staring straight at her.

'I know,' was all she could summon to say. 'I wish you had too.'

'Did you miss me?'

Stupid question, Harry.

'That's not a fair question.'

'I know, but I'm asking it anyway. Answer it, please.'

Answer it, he says. Hell, I could write a book about it. What the heck do I say? Do I tell him the truth, that I missed him every day? That I sobbed at every sonogram appointment? That I once punched an advert on the wall of the Tube station because it had an advertisement for Dubai on it? No, no, no. Protect that underbelly, Sanders. Don't give everything away.

'Well, yes. Short answer, I did miss you, for a long time.'

For ever, in fact. You ruined me for all other men. No, not that either. You sound like an old maid.

She took another sip of her wine and started to talk. 'I vomited. In the airport. Did you know that? All over the airport lounge. Pregnancy joys, I guess, but I didn't know at the time.'

He shook his head, his expression giving nothing away. She waved him off with her hand.

'Of course you didn't. Sorry. It was after you'd gone. I threw up right there in the check-in hall, in front of everyone. The woman behind the counter got a shock, I can tell you.'

'I'm sorry for that.'

'I threw up because I was already pregnant with Aidan. I didn't know at the time, not till a few weeks after. I ignored the signs, I suppose, or more I didn't see them. The possibility didn't enter my head. Even with all my training, I didn't have a clue.'

Harry hung his head, a look she'd never seen before on his face. 'Sometimes, even the best training in the world can't make you see the signs that are right there in front of you. Not till the body takes over and makes you see it. None of this is your fault. Did you ever hate me?'

'Who says I don't now?' she quipped, but he didn't laugh. 'No, I never hated you. We had a child coming. I had no room in my heart for hate.'

'Did you miss me all the time?'

He was looking at her intently, his eyes focused on her. Her eyes, then her lips. She licked them without thinking, feeling suddenly parched. She took another sip of Dutch courage, and she could feel Harry tense at the side of her when she took too long to answer. As though doubt had crept into the silence and filled it for him.

'Sorry. Forget I asked. I didn't mean to push.'

'Yes,' she admitted finally. 'I missed you every day. I missed telling you about work, about the funny things that happened in the station. When Aidan took his first steps, I cried myself to sleep. When I was in labour, Tom at my side, I shouted for you to come. He told me after. I was delirious on gas and air, half out of my mind with pain and fear. I missed you Harry; we all did.' She turned back to the television and heard the clink of his wine glass on the coffee table. Felt him take her glass from her hand. She kept her eyes on the television, feeling as if every nerve-ending was on fire.

'Look at me, Annie. Please.' For once, hearing his name for her didn't make her feel anything but cherished. She was still his Annie.

She took a breath and turned to him. He was closer now, his face inches from hers.

'I'm glad I told you why I left. I wanted you to know. To understand why I made the mistake of not taking you with me. I missed you too. I loved you so much, Annie. Every single day. Your face kept me going on my worst days. I threw up a lot too, when I was sick. I regret a lot in my life, but nothing quite so much as how much I hurt you. How I wrecked our little family before it had even begun. The thing is, I—'

'Do you still?'

Her question threw him off track, and he tried to stay on subject. Being so close to her after all this time was intoxicating. It made his head spin. Her lips were so close, her body turned to him as her face searched his for the answer she sought. He was trying to get his lips to work, to form the sounds he was desperate to get out there, but all the treacherous things wanted to do was meet with hers. He wanted to kiss her stupid, and they tingled with the sheer need. Damn his body; it had let him down at some of the most pivotal moments. You never learned that in any textbook.

'Do I still what?' He finally managed to get them back under control.

Looking at him now, she looked like the young girl he had fallen in love with. Strong, driven, but less sure of herself.

'Love me.'

That was the easiest question to answer. It had never been in doubt, all these years. It had never dulled. Not over time or the thousands of miles, or even when he'd been fighting against the bad cells that were within him, trying to take him away from her for good. Throughout all that, she had been the voice in his head, his reason for getting up and facing each day. Every day—from the day in the airport to this one. Till the day he finally left this earth.

'Yes, Annie. God, yes.' He took her hands in his, rubbing his thumbs along the soft skin he'd once thought he'd never get to touch again. 'I never stopped. Never.'

She closed the gap between them and he met her there. Their lips melded together as they poured every ounce of their love into their kiss. He lifted her into his arms and she straddled him on the sofa, her hair falling over them both as they explored each other's mouths. Harry could feel her heart pumping fast, every bit as fast as his.

She broke off the kiss to draw breath. 'I love you too, Harry. Damn you, but I love you too.'

CHAPTER SIX

THE IMPOSING BRICK building of the inner-city primary school loomed in Harry's windshield as they pulled into the car park. He'd driven the whole way from her house with her hand in his lap, his hand covering hers between every change of gear. He'd even grumbled about that, declaring his intention to take back his hire car the second he got the chance and buy a car with automatic gears, so he didn't have to let go of her hand.

Annabel couldn't argue with that. She loved every minute of the time they spent together—the minutes they were alone, away from prying eyes. Since the fateful movie night, they'd been meeting out of work whenever they got a chance, and a babysitter. He'd taken her to Chinatown and watched her demolish half the menu with a big daft grin on his face. They'd kissed in the cinema like a pair of teenagers, all thoughts of the action flick forgotten as they held each other in the dark.

They'd never taken it further than that, though it was getting harder to call time on their kissing. Without even discussing it, they'd both seemingly reached the same conclusion. They were taking their time, the pair of them seeing how fragile this new relationship was, how much was at stake. At work, they'd still been the same team, all thoughts of the past put to bed, or left unsaid. She knew that they'd never finished their conversation, that he had more to say, but at this moment in her life she was content to stay in their bubble.

Harry had spent time with Aidan too, at the house, but they'd told no one about the development in their relationship. They'd been careful around Aidan, but once he was in bed their couch kissing sessions made her feel like a young teenager in love all over again. And she was kissing the same boy, who was now the hottest man she'd ever laid eyes on. She could admit that to herself fully now she was done being mad at him. Not that she needed to. Her wandering hands were testament to that. She was surprised they hadn't set her new couch on fire with the intensity of their barely contained heat. Amazing what a kiss could do to wake a girl up from a deep sleep. She was well and truly awake now, and she felt beautiful. Seen.

Sometimes, when they were walking down the corridor at work towards each other, acting professional, he would give her a look, or she would feel him brush against her skin, and she felt so deliciously high, naughty even. As professional as they kept things, hiding the development in their relationship from everyone around them, she felt as if they were walking around in their own bubble. Whenever he was near her, she felt his presence. She glowed like a star in the night sky and, judging by his fumbling sometimes, the way he tripped over his words, she knew she wasn't the only one lighting up. She just didn't want anyone else to see it. Not yet.

They didn't need any opinions from those around them. They'd not even discussed where it was going. Annabel wasn't going to be the one to push it. She wasn't even sure herself what they were doing, but it felt right. They'd spent their rare weekends off together at Annabel's house, cooking meals together and dancing in the kitchen. He'd rocked up one day with a football net for Aidan, and they'd barbecued outside in the newly finished garden, Harry being the goalie to Aidan's striker. She'd never laughed so much, and Aidan was thrilled with having a man around the house.

It could be like this all the time, she thought to herself for the millionth time. *If you just let go, let all the truths blow away with the wind, we could be happy. We could be a family.*

He was still the same tender, loving Harry he'd been before, better even, but there were times when he grew quiet. He avoided going into too much detail about his illness, how bad it had actually been. It must have changed him, and she wondered whether he was truly happy being back, especially when he seemed so far away in his own head at times. She wondered what he was thinking, whether he was longing for far-off shores again. Was he really as recovered as he said he was? She didn't want to rock the boat, but she had a million questions. It was such a nice time sailing through life with him, so she gave him time.

The murmurs around the station were still there; she caught the odd look when they walked in together, chatting away to each other, but she held her head high and pretended that she didn't. She was the head paramedic; her position was one of integrity, and they were doing nothing wrong. At work, other than the fizz in her belly, she was always on the ball. She would never let a patient down; neither of them ever would. Medicine and patient care meant far too much to both of them. Once she had a label for what they were, other than childhood sweethearts and secret co-parents, then that would be a different matter. Work would have to know. She was still in control of her career, and that would never change.

Harry turned off the engine and looked out at the school. 'It looks nice.'

Distracted, she glanced at the school and smiled.

'Yeah, he loves it here. He's got lots of friends too. He wants to be a paramedic, you know.'

Harry's eyebrows shot up to his hairline. 'Really? That's great! A chip off the old block, eh? Dad will be furious.'

They laughed together, thinking of Abe.

'I think we should tell him,' she said softly.

'Rather you than me; he's already talking about getting him a doctor play set for Christmas.'

'No, not Abe.' She pulled his hand to her mouth, kissing the back. 'Aidan. I think we should tell him that you're his father.'

Harry didn't reply for a moment, but his expression said everything. His eyes brimmed with tears and he blinked, seemingly to push them back.

'Are you sure?'

'Yes, I'm sure. We're all spending so much time together, and I feel so guilty for keeping it from him. You do everything a dad does, Harry. You play with him, look after him— you're in his life. He deserves a real father, not some abstract faraway idea of you. I've taken enough time from you both. Enough now—we can be a proper family. No more hiding.'

Harry was moving his head like a nodding dog now, his grip on her hand tight. 'When?'

'Today, after school. We can take him to the park, tell him then.' Annabel stroked his face, which was now rather pale. 'You freaking out?'

He silenced her with an enthusiastic kiss. 'Hell, no. I'm ready.' His features clouded again. 'Does this mean telling him about us too?'

'I hadn't thought that far, in all honesty, but yes, I think so. One thing at a time, maybe. Let's do this first. See how he copes.'

'He'll have questions. What do I tell him?'

'The truth, as much as we can. You went to help people, to save lives. He'll understand that. Every adult around him is a professional lifesaver. We can tell him everything when he's older. He's always coped okay, understood that his dad wasn't around.' That was true, though she had seen him get upset sometimes. Father's Day. Christmas. Seeing other dads at the school gates. She didn't tell Harry any of that. It didn't need to be said. It would only serve to torture them both. 'You're here now. Things are different.'

There it was again. That faraway look.

'I want that more than anything, but we need to talk too. Before we go any further. I have things to tell you. I know I don't talk about my cancer much, but I do have more things to say.'

'We should go in,' she said, checking her watch. 'It starts soon; he'll be waiting.'

'You're doing it again.'

'I'm not.'

I am. I'm scared. What if I don't like the answer? What if he gets sick again, like Mum?

'We need to get in there. Aidan's waiting.'

'I can't have children, Annie. The cancer treatment was really intense, and at the time they offered to freeze some of my semen, but I was just too upset. I never wanted a child once I'd lost you. Another stupid regret of mine. I should have stuck some of those little soldiers on ice.'

The statement hung in the air between them. She felt as if it had slapped her in the face. Hard.

'That's not funny.'

'Do you see me laughing?'

'We have Aidan though. I guessed that your cancer might have left you sterile. Hell, I've done enough research over the last few weeks, I'll admit. What are you saying?'

'Aidan is mine. I'm not questioning that. I'm saying that I can't have children.'

'I don't understand. I haven't mentioned having another child. Does it bother you?'

'You're not listening again. It's not about wanting another child. I love Aidan. You know that. I'm telling you that I can't father a child.'

Harry sighed, and she knew he'd seen her check her watch again. In truth, she wanted to jump out of the car, avoid the conversation altogether. Was he changing his mind about them?

'Okay, Miss Punctual. The short version is that treatment was pretty intensive. It was touch and go for a while. They asked me if I wanted to freeze my sperm at the time but, with losing you, I just didn't see the point. Another thing I wish I'd thought better of. The upshot is, I'm sterile. Have been for about six years now. I've been wanting to tell you since I got back. Since we got back together. I need you to know, before we tell Aidan anything. What if we become a family, and you want more kids? I can't give you that. Everything else, yes, God, yes, but not that. I couldn't lose you again.'

Annabel felt upset, but not for herself. More for him. He'd been carrying this a long time; she could see on his face that he was terrified of her reaction. She could at least calm him down on that score. She'd known he was hiding something, and her relief was palpable. She didn't care; she'd made peace with it since that day at the house. She'd known the treatments, the prognosis, the complications that often occurred. Since her mother got sick, cancer had become her specialist subject.

'I've never thought about having more children. I'm happy at work, Aidan is thriving.

We have you. Why worry about something when we don't have to?'

'You say that now, but—'

'But nothing. I love Aidan with all of my heart, but he's enough. More than enough. Hell, I don't even think I could do that again. Does it bother you?'

'I've made peace with it. I guess you can't really miss what you don't have, and I didn't have you either. I always imagined us having a family. When I found out about Aidan, it felt surreal. In a good way.' He was rushing his words out now, and Annabel sat and listened. 'I never thought I'd be a father. Being a father to your child, Annie? It's everything. He's the cherry on the top of my coming home.'

Annabel smiled, taking his face between her hands and pulling him in for a lingering kiss. Out of the corner of her eye she saw movement through the window. Kids' heads bobbing up and down.

'We need to go, but you don't need to worry, Harry. We *are* a family. You coming home completed that for me. And besides, Aidan's been dropping hints about a dog. If we get broody we can expand that way.' She smirked at him, and his face finally relaxed.

'Okay, but we need to talk about this some more. It's a lot to ask of you.'

'Don't you always want to talk?' she deflected expertly, sticking her tongue out at him to lighten the mood. 'You're not asking anything of me, Harry. I have my family. I'm happy, finally.' She kissed him again. 'Come on, we have an audience to wow.'

Aidan's smile was so big that it filled his whole face as the two paramedics gave their talk, telling the children about their day-to-day duties. Leaving out the scary stuff, and telling a few stories about rescuing people from railings, helped by other emergency services, about how fast the ambulance went, how cool it was to help the people of London. Harry talked of Dubai, the people he'd met there, the way their medical systems ran differently to those in England. How sweaty it could get out there, what his days off looked like. The children were like little sponges, absorbing every word, and sticking their hands up to ask more questions. The other parents even asked a few of their own.

All too soon, though, the school bell went and the children all said goodbye to their parents and started to file out of the classroom. Mrs Shepherd, the class teacher, was left sitting at her desk, marking papers. Before long, it was just the four of them.

'Well, kiddo, I think that went well.' Annabel gave Aidan a sneaky hug and, for once in a public setting, he allowed it.

'Are you kidding? It was amazing!' He threw his arms out wide, making a rainbow-shaped arc with his hands. 'Thank you, thank you, thank you!' He hugged Harry's legs tight.

Mrs Shepherd came across the room. 'Sorry to interrupt. Aidan, you need to get out to break now. You can show them to reception if you like, but then straight outside for some fresh air.' She gave Annabel a friendly nod. 'Nice to see you again.'

'You too. Come on then, kiddo, you're missing your football time.'

Aidan walked them both to reception, holding one hand of each of them, keeping up a constant stream of chatter all the way. Harry winked at Annabel over his head, and she winked back. She really felt as if things were falling into place. Even with his bombshell. They just needed tonight to go well, and another barrier would be broken down.

'Fancy the park tonight, after school? We have the day off; we could get ice-cream?'

'Harry too?' he asked, moving his hands from side to side, taking them along with him.

'Who do you think wants the ice-cream?' Harry laughed.

They reached reception and said goodbye to Aidan. His friend was just coming out of the toilets, and as Harry and Annabel signed out of the visitors book and waited for the school office to buzz them out of the secure entrance they heard the boys chatting.

'You coming out to play football, Aidy? Miss said we could use the top field.'

'Yeah, coming, Joey.' The boy he called Joey looked at the two adults, who were watching the receptionist finish up a call behind the glass screen. She'd given them 'one minute' with the raising of a finger.

'Who's that with your mum?' the boy asked, curiosity on his face.

'Oh, that's Harry,' Aidan said. 'He's a paramedic like Mum. They work together.'

The receptionist put down the receiver and the door buzzed. They were almost out of the door when they heard something else before the two boys ran off to the doors to the playground.

'That's so cool,' Joey said, a hint of wonder in his voice.

'I know,' Aidan replied, pride evident in his tone. 'And he's my dad too. He finally came home.'

Annabel and Harry didn't say a word until they were back in the car, and Harry was pulling away towards Abe's house, where they were due for lunch.

'Well,' Annabel said eventually, shock vibrating through her, 'I guess he'll take the news in his stride. Do they sell gin-flavoured ice-cream at the park?'

* * *

The late afternoon sun fell in shimmering spots along the grass as they sat on a bench together. The three of them were each holding cones of ice cream of different flavours—bubblegum for Aidan, rum and raisin for Harry and Annabel. The closest thing she could get to gin in ice-cream form. Aidan's lips were coated in blue sparkly dust, and a short distance away children whooped and shrieked in delight as they swung on metal swings and pushed each other around on the spinning roundabout.

Harry's phone rang and, after taking it out of his pocket to look at the screen, he silenced the call and shoved it back into his jacket. Annabel frowned, but said nothing. It wasn't the time, but she noticed that even since he'd told her about his fertility the clouds had not completely disappeared from over his head. Come to think of it, he'd had a couple of calls the last few days, with the same response and mood afterwards.

'Aidan, when we were leaving your school

today, we heard you speaking to your friend Joey—do you remember?'

Aidan paused mid lick, his eyes going wide. Annabel could see his eyes dart from side to side, assessing their facial expressions.

'You're not in trouble; you know that, right?' She looked to Harry for support, but he was staring off into the distance, seemingly deep in thought. She frowned in his direction but focused back on Aidan. 'You said something to him, and we just wanted to know what you thought.'

'About Harry?' he said between licks of his cornet. He was a little less enthusiastic attacking the iced treat now. At the side of him, Harry seemed to come to at the sound of his name, and Annabel gave him a nod. She thought he should take the lead. He'd missed enough moments. This one should belong to him. He took the cue, and addressed the little boy sitting between them.

'You said that you thought I might be your father. Did that come from somewhere? Did you hear it somewhere?'

Aidan had stopped eating now, his head

down, and Harry put his arm around him. His phone rang again in his pocket, and he cursed under his breath before shutting it off altogether. He never moved the arm that was wrapped around his son. Annabel caught him looking at him.

He's acting strange. Even in the current circumstances.

'Shall I go get us a drink from the stand?' she asked, giving him an opportunity to talk to Aidan alone if he needed it. And herself a minute to worry about the phone calls. Was it Dubai, wanting him back? He wouldn't go now, surely?

'In a minute, perhaps,' he said softly, touching her shoulder with the arm that hung around Aidan's sheepish form. 'Aidan?'

'I guessed,' Aidan said eventually. 'Mummy only has photos of you at home, none of my dad, and you went away to work. Saving people. I thought maybe that's why you couldn't be here, because you had to help people far away. Granddad isn't Mum's daddy, because he isn't here, so I guessed he might be your dad. When we did our family tree project at school, Miss Shepherd said something, and I thought that might make you my dad. I got to ask the teacher lots of questions. I came top of the class.'

The expression on both adults' features was one of shocked wonder.

'Have you known for a long time?' Annabel said, a tear dropping down her cheek when she thought of her little boy being so clever, searching for answers like a little detective.

Aidan wiped it away. 'Yes, I think so. You used to get all weird when you looked at his photos at Granddad's. Don't cry, Mum. My mates are over there. It's well embarrassing.'

She laughed through her sobs, trying to get a grip but only managing to reduce herself to a snotty mess. Harry produced a pack of tissues from his pocket and passed them across with a smile.

'I figured,' he quipped. Looking straight at Aidan, his face lit up.

'It's true, Aidan, I am your dad— Oof!'

He was cut off by Aidan flinging himself into his chest, wrapping his arms around him. A smear of blue ice-cream stained Harry's top, but he didn't even notice. He hugged Aidan back, before lifting his chin to meet his eyes.

'I am your dad, but I didn't know I was your dad when I went away. The thing is, something happened, and I didn't treat your mum very well. I broke her heart, and so she protected you from getting your heart broken too. I'm sorry for that, Aidan, but I'm here now and I want to make it right. Grown-ups aren't very smart sometimes. Not as smart as you, anyway.' Aidan grinned at that.

'I came back to mend what I broke, and when I found out about you I was so happy.' He was smiling now, his eyes glistening with tears of his own. 'I should have been there for you, Aidan, but I wasn't, and that breaks *my* heart. We wanted to tell you today, actually, right here, but you beat us to it.'

The two males mirrored each other with their lopsided grins, and Annabel sobbed again.

'Mum!'

'Annie! It's okay!'

Annabel groaned, trying to pull herself together.

'Sorry, sorry! I'll go get the drinks, okay?' She stood up off the bench, giving them both a watery-eyed wave before heading over to the small crowd of people at the refreshments stand.

The two of them were left alone now, listening to the chatter of people around them.

'Are you mad at Mum, for not telling you?' Aidan's voice was curious, and Harry marvelled at the little character he'd helped create.

Harry shook his head. 'When I left, I didn't make it easy on her. I could never be mad. I love her, just like you do. You shouldn't be mad at her either. It was your mum who asked me to come home, and she told me about you.'

'Are you going to go away again?' Aidan's ice-cream was nothing but a small cone of wafer in his hand now, his little fingers sticky and stained blue.

Harry thought of the phone calls he'd received earlier. He recognised the number; he knew that they wouldn't be calling unless they had something important to say. He took a deep breath and tipped the rest of his own cone into the bin next to the bench. He didn't want to lie to his son. He wanted to be the parent who was there, who showed up, who Aidan could trust. He chose his next words carefully.

'There's nowhere I'd rather be than with you and your mum, and that's the truth. I'm happy to be here.'

Annabel was slowly walking back towards them now, and he winked at her as she approached. He mouthed 'I love you' to her, and she said it back, her troubled expression relaxing as she came closer to the bench.

'Good,' Aidan said. 'Now we just have to make Mum let you move in. We have a big house now, and Mum's garbage at football. We could play every day!'

He dropped a kiss on the top of his son's head, chuckling. The phone calls could wait. He didn't want anything to spoil the day. He wanted to focus on claiming his family and shouting from the rooftops that he was the father of this wonderful boy. The son of the love of his life, past and present. It was the future that had a question mark over it, hanging like the reaper's scythe over his head. One thing Harry was sure of: he was used to fighting, and this would be no different.

CHAPTER SEVEN

ONCE AIDAN HAD digested their talk, and many talks after in the days that followed, and Abe was in the picture, they let the dust settle and enjoyed life in their new groove for a while, until they decided that today, finally, was the day.

In truth, Annabel had been the one to beg Harry to take the plunge professionally. For some reason, he'd still been a little quiet. A little too cautious. Their nights on the couch were always full of hot kisses and tender caresses, but Harry was steadfast in making them wait. A little voice inside her head had been asking questions she didn't like the sound of. Tiny dandelion seeds of doubt were threatening to blow over their new lives, which felt like sunny, cloudless days in the park. Till now, when he'd been the one to pick the day.

When they were both finished on shift and changed, they headed to HR to declare their relationship. It was just a formality, needed to cover against possible sexual harassment claims in the future. Things could turn sour in matters of the heart, and the hospital, as any other business, protected itself from any fallout.

It wasn't uncommon for staff to date each other; with their hours and shift patterns, their dating pool wasn't exactly swimming with fish. Being together in those high-pressure situations, you really got to know a person. Tonight, they were going to know each other even better.

'All done,' Annabel said, puffing out a sigh of relief as they headed out of the hospital. 'Are you sure Abe will be okay with having Aidan for the whole night on a school night? I could have arranged a sleepover at one of his friend's houses, I'm sure.'

'Don't be daft; they were thrilled. He's probably going to grill the teachers on what science lessons they're giving the kids on the morning drop-off.' Harry stopped her in the foyer, turning her to face him and taking her into his arms. She looked around her to check for onlookers. 'And stop doing that too. We're official now, remember? HR certified to hold each other in the corridors. And other things out of work.' His look was positively devilish, and she couldn't help but giggle.

'Down, boy.'

Harry seemed brighter today, the melancholy that settled over him sometimes seemingly gone. The phone calls had stopped too, but it worried her what that meant. Still, making things official was good.

What else can he possibly have to hide? Unless he is secretly James Bond, we're good now. Nothing can break us apart.

'Hey, it's been a long time. We've waited enough. I've been back a long time now. We have the entire night to go out, drink, eat some fast congealing buffet food, and act like a couple. In public. With an empty house and a huge bed to get back to.'

The butterflies in her stomach were doing

back flips off her ribcage now, and she had to shut her thoughts down. Till later anyway. She had changed her sheets and might just have had a wax. A girl had to prepare, after all.

'I'm going to miss Purdie though; she's been there from the beginning. It will be weird not seeing her on the wards.'

'I know. She's been a good friend to both of us. Especially since I got back.' His smile faded a little, but he soon recovered. 'The oncology department won't be the same without her.' He caught sight of the clock on the wall behind her, and steered them both in the direction of the car park.

'Come on, let's go. First tequila is on me.'

He was wearing a dark blue shirt, paired with a pair of jeans that made Annabel drag her feet just a little bit, so she could watch his gorgeous bum in action as they headed to the party for Purdie. She was retiring, and not just retiring to stay home and knit. Her daughters had returned to Barbados, and she was jetting off next week to be reunited with them. To enjoy her well-earned twilight years and sit in the sun, watching her grandchildren grow up. Annabel was nothing but happy for her. Family was everything in this life, which they all knew could be short, and cruel.

The bar was nothing fancy, Purdie's colleagues opting for a private room in the back so that Purdie would be centre stage for her going away party. They pulled up in the black cab, Harry passing the driver some notes and taking Annabel's hand as they stepped out into the London night. There was nothing like her home city when the sun went down. The atmosphere was always one of excitement, the bustle of people in suits heading for after dinner drinks, celebrating birthdays, promotions and big deals being done. She loved living here, even when the calls and the pressures of her job brought her to her exhausted knees. Now Harry was here, everything seemed that bit brighter.

The second they walked into the already lively events room, Harry's hand gripped hers.

'Are you ready for this?' she asked him

gently. 'Our first night out of the medical supply closet?'

He chuckled, rubbing his thumb along her palm.

'Let's go get a drink,' Harry replied in her ear, making her shiver slightly.

Purdie was already there, looking lovely in a pretty dark red velvet dress. She was standing a little way away, chatting to some of their colleagues. She looked over, and Annabel gave her a wave. She waved back, but she looked distracted, her eyes flicking from Harry to hers. Annabel shook off the uneasy feeling it gave her. Something wasn't quite right; she could feel it. She let go of Harry's hand and caught the barman's attention. She needed a stiff drink to bolster her confidence.

'Everything okay?' Purdie walked over to them as they headed over to a vacant table. 'I see the nurses are on form tonight.' Some of the oncology nurses were sitting at a table, cackling loudly and thoroughly enjoying themselves.

'Work hard, play hard.' Harry laughed. Purdie laughed too, but it sounded forced in Annabel's ears. She eyed Harry, and something in that look had Annabel's Spidey sense tingling.

'You okay, Harrison?' Purdie asked him, her professional voice in full flow now.

'I'm fine,' Harry said shortly. 'You should be enjoying your party.'

'Oh, child, I intend to.' She looked at Annabel, who was watching them both like a tennis spectator. 'You two finally got your act together, didn't you! I'm so glad! I was planning on locking you in one of the offices before I left. You've wasted enough time.'

'Yes, you're right there,' Annabel said, laughing now. Harry spotted someone, frowning, and he made his apologies and left, leaving the two of them alone. She took advantage of the moment. 'He's Aidan's dad too. His biological father.'

Purdie laughed then, a loud, joyous laugh. 'Oh, I knew that! Come on, you think anything misses my attention around that hospital? Please.' She pulled Annabel in for a perfume-soaked hug. 'I'm so happy for you all. It makes my heart glad. You want a holiday, you come to Barbados. Aidan will play with my grandbabies, we can drink cocktails and watch them play.'

'Now that sounds like a plan.' Annabel laughed, noticing that Harry was speaking to the head of oncology. The way they were huddled together, serious expressions focused on each other, had everything in her switch to full panic mode. The phone calls, the way he'd been acting…

She strode over and caught the tail-end of the conversation before the two men realised that she was standing there.

Dr Geller was speaking. 'With that type of chemo, I'm afraid the prognosis is not good at all. I'm sorry, Harry.'

Annabel felt as if her heart had fallen out of her heels. The room swayed. She knew what the consultant meant. She'd seen it enough times in her career, had had to watch her full-of-life mother fade away to nearly nothing. Everything fell into place. The secretive phone calls. Harry's sombre moods. Delaying their intimacy this long. She looked at Harry, waiting for him to refute the jigsaw pieces that were slotting together in her mind, but he just looked at her, stricken.

'It's true, isn't it? You're sick again,' she said. 'Aren't you? It makes sense now. The phone calls, the moods.' Another thought slammed into her shocked thought pattern, scattering whatever control she had over her words. 'That's why you came back. Not for me at all. You came back because you got sick again.' She laughed, a hollow sound from deep in her gut, shock and terror rippling through her. The tears were already escaping. She looked at her surroundings, aware that she was with her subordinates and friends. The pain of her old humiliation reared its ugly head.

I am such an idiot. He didn't come back for me. He came back six months after my call. He came home to make amends before he died.

It seemed so surreal, but she'd heard Dr Geller's words.

'I can't do this. Not again.'

'You can't do what? Annie, let's go outside. I'll explain.' Dr Geller had melted into the crowd, obviously eager to avoid the scene that was about to happen. She was trying to calm down, but she just couldn't stop her mind from going to the worst, darkest places. Aidan loved him; they were together. He'd lied about his cancer all over again.

Oh, dear God. I'm going to lose him. For ever this time.

Harry was trying to reach for her hands, but she felt her anger rise and she shoved him away from her, as hard as she could. His hands fell to his sides, defeated.

'Just listen, Annie, please. Let's go back to yours; we can talk.'

'I can't believe I fell for your lies again! I told Aidan about you! You let me love you again! Why would you do that? I watched my mother die! A horrible, painful death.' She was sobbing now, smearing her make-up as she tried to wipe away the tears that were blurring her vision. 'Aidan!' Her broken-hearted humiliation turned to white-hot rage. 'You want Aidan to go through that? You're a selfish bastard, Harry, I hate you.

Why would you keep this from me again? Why don't you trust me?'

'No, Annie, I'm—'

'No, Harry, I'm done listening to you. Done. I never should have trusted you.'

He had tears in his eyes too now, his hands limp at his sides. 'Stop, Annie, this is so stupid.'

'Stupid, eh? Screw you, Harry.'

Before she was even aware of what she was doing, she was sitting in the back of a cab, heels in her shaking hand. Just as it pulled away, she saw Harry run out into the street after her, stopping traffic while Purdie stood in the doorway of the bar. Car horns honked, but Harry was oblivious.

'Annie!' she could hear him shout after her. 'Annie, please! Stop! I love you!'

The driver turned to her, slowing down. 'You Annie? You want me to stop?'

She reached for her bag, wanting to ring Abe, to warn him that she didn't want Harry around Aidan. She didn't want Abe to be left in the dark again either, but she knew if she turned up to collect Aidan like this, smelling of tequila and looking like a fan at an Alice Cooper concert, it would upset them both far more. She realised she'd left her bag behind, in her rush to escape. She heard Harry shout her name again, and she covered her ears.

She reeled off her address to the cab driver. She had cash at home to pay him at the other end.

'No, please, just drive. Can you step on it, please?'

The cab driver looked as if he wanted to ask more, but he just nodded and discreetly closed the glass partition between them. The lights of the city streets flickered through the windows as they joined the evening flow of London traffic.

She processed everything from the evening, the last few weeks even, through fresh eyes. Filtering through the past few weeks with the new information applied as an overlay.

Harry is sick. Cancer sick. Possibly dying sick.

Her gut twisted and she felt as if her heart, newly whole, was fighting to keep the blood pumping around her body. She thought of her mother, the vibrant, strong single parent who had raised her to be the woman she was today. In her final days, her mother had been unrecognisable from the strong woman she'd been. The fire had still been there, but stifled by the cancer, and the treatment that had ultimately failed to save her.

Annabel cried fresh tears as the long-forgotten memory burned in her brain. She thought of growing up, just the two of them together. She'd had a great childhood, but a lonely one at times. Could she deprive Aidan of that chance, even after everything that had happened? Even if the reality could be short, and painful? She thought of how Aidan would feel if he knew that she had kept him from those final moments with the father he had just found, however hard they might be. She didn't want him to miss another moment. And, truthfully, she didn't want to waste any more time either. She loved Harry, and she'd been apart from him for far too long already. They all had.

What was more, she had just been horrible to him. In her shock and pain, she'd never even thought about how scared he must be feeling, about how he had made the same mistake again, not telling her to protect her. He loved her so much, he didn't want to share the pain. She was the worst woman in the world. She'd left him there, humiliated him. Just like she had felt in that stupid airport. She was so disgusted with herself.

She pulled up to the house, which was in darkness apart from the light she'd left on in the hallway. It really was looking great now, everything she'd dreamed of for all these years. A family home.

She smiled at the driver. 'I'm sorry, I won't be a minute. I left my purse behind at the bar.'

The driver nodded, and she then realised that her keys were also in her bag. Thank God for the hidden key she'd kept for when she wasn't there and Aidan needed to get in with her friend Teri. She picked her heels up from the cab floor and went around the side of the house, picking up the plant pot of flowers that she kept it under. She was just coming out of the house, money in hand, when her taxi pulled away.

'Hey, wait! I have your money!'

'I paid it,' a voice said from the darkness of the street. She heard footsteps, and Harry stepped out from the shadows, lit by the nearby streetlight. 'I came to talk.'

She saw her purse in his hands. 'Oh, thank God, my whole life is in there.'

'Not quite,' he said, slowly walking up the path. She met him step for step. 'You were in a hurry.'

'I know. I am so sorry I did that. I feel awful. I was just going to call you, ask you to come over.'

He halted. 'Really?'

She kept walking towards him till they were standing in front of each other. He had hope etched across his drained features now, and she wanted to just take him into her arms and hold him. Heal him.

Oh, the irony.

He held her purse out to her, and she took it from him and dropped it to the side on the wet grass.

'Really, now let me get this out. I care that you lied, and that was the last time, Harry. If we're going to do this, and I mean really do this, then you need to be honest with me. One more half-truth, however small you think it is, I'm out. And so is Aidan. So help me God, I could kick your ass, but I understand why you didn't want to tell me.'

He went to speak, but she gently touched her palms to his chest. He felt warm to the touch, and she realised how cold she'd felt since leaving his side.

'It's my turn to speak. I love you, Harrison Abraham Carter. I love every hair on your stupid, stupid head. I love that we made our son together, and that you are the man in a storm at work, and at home. These last few months have been—'

'Challenging?' he offered. She nodded, a sliver of a smile passing across her features.

'Challenging, annoying, terrifying. All of those too, but I was going to say amazing. I love you; I've loved you since I was a green as grass medical student, not knowing one end of an IV from the other, and I love you now. I'm glad you came home. I've felt more alive since you returned than I have in years.

I guess I blocked a lot out because it was just too difficult to face. I never let you speak, but I am listening.'

'Can I speak yet?'

'No.' She bent down on one knee, right there on the moonlit path, and looked up at him.

'Harrison Abraham Carter, I don't have a ring but take these words as my vow. Marry me. Be my husband, for however long we have. For ever, hopefully, but I'll settle for any days the big man upstairs can give us. Make this fight our fight and be by my side. In sickness and in health.'

Harry brushed away a tear and knelt down with her.

'Annie, I'm not sick. I got the all-clear a long time ago. I went for a check-up when I got back to London. After our talk, I went to get my fertility checked. Just so I had the full picture. It's what I thought. That's what Dr Geller was telling me. With my treatment, it was never likely, but I wanted to be sure before I told you. Truly, Annie, I'm going nowhere. Ever again.'

Annie's breaths came thick and fast, her lungs gasping for air as she looked at the man before her.

'Oh, my God, I'm such an idiot. I made such a scene. I don't care about having more children. I meant that when I said it before. We have Aidan, and each other. We can adopt a whole house full of kids if you want. I don't care, Harry. I just want to be a family. I always wanted that.'

He stood, taking her with him. 'That's all I want.' He dipped down, getting down on one knee himself now and pulling a ring box out of his pocket. 'I was planning to do this tonight anyway but, as usual, I can't get a word in.' He opened the box, and there sat a beautiful ring. It was stunning, the jewels shining in the moonlight. 'I bought this ring six months ago, in Dubai. When you called, and I was coming back to you, I saw this in a shop window and I knew that if I ever got the chance to be with you again I wouldn't wait a moment. I wanted to be ready. Annabel Sanders, will you please be my wife? My Annie, for ever?'

Annabel was crying, her whole body shaking as she nodded and put out her hand. He put the ring on her finger and kissed it.

'I love you, Annie.'

'I love you too, Harry. I'm so sorry that we missed out on so much. You missed out on being a father for so long, but from today we can put all this right. Be together.'

Harry stood and, taking her into his strong arms, he kissed her with everything he had. She kissed him right back, not quite believing she was in his arms again. 'Let's get inside.' He wrapped his arm around her and they headed to the light coming from the doorway. 'We have a lot of time to make up for.'

He flashed her a devilish grin, and she laughed as he took her into his arms, heading towards the open door. They were finally where they wanted to be. They were home.

EPILOGUE

'So, love of my life, how do you like Dubai?'

Harry's voice behind her only momentarily distracted her from the view. She couldn't quite believe her eyes; the photos that her new husband had shown her hadn't done the beauty of the land nearly enough justice. It felt worlds away from London and the home her little family all now lived in together. Standing out on the balcony of their hotel suite, Aidan asleep in the adjoining room, being watched over by Abe, she sighed happily.

'I can't quite believe we're here. Together.'

'I know.' His arms wrapped around her waist and she felt the stubble on his cheek graze her neck, making her shiver, even in the heat of the night. 'I'm so glad we got to come here. I thought about it a lot when I was here, away from you all.'

'Only took us a decade.' She laughed.

'Well, you kept me dangling on the engagement hook long enough!' he teased, an old running joke between them now.

'Hey!' She slapped gently at one of the hands around her, and he nuzzled his scruff in deeper, scraping it along her cheek, making her laugh and shiver with lust, all at the same time. 'I'll have you know I am a busy career woman with a very full schedule.'

He growled, turning her to face him and kissing her impulsively. 'That's it, keep talking. Tell me all about it; I love a strong woman.'

She giggled, wrapping her arms around the back of his head, running her fingers through his thick hair. They had music playing from the corner of the lavish room, and a familiar song came on. Slowly, they started to sway together, enjoying the solitude after their busy day out sightseeing.

They'd even been to the hospital where Harry had worked, and Abe, Aidan and Annie had all loved meeting Harry's friends and colleagues, seeing just how much he was loved, how he'd been missed. They could all relate to missing Harry. They'd even met the doctors and nurses who had helped treat him for the aggressive cancer he'd arrived with. Annie had cried then, hugging more than one of them a little too tightly, and thanking them over and over. They knew all about her, which was probably the most surprising thing of all. Looking at Harry's proud and slightly embarrassed face, she knew she'd fallen in love with him even more right then and there. Something she'd never thought possible since that day they had met again in the airport car park. Even then, her heart had come back to life. Even through the hurt, and the anger at his departure.

Their colleagues had all been amazing. They were all thrilled for them, and the news about Harry being Aidan's real father had been met with happiness too, and more than a few knowing looks. She loved them all even more for keeping their suspicions to themselves, making those early years easier to bear. There were no secrets now, and the station was a happier place for it.

Purdie was happy with the result too. She video called them often, and Aidan was getting to know her family right along with them. Barbados was next on the holiday list, and they had already done Spain and most of the British tourist attractions. The days out as a family had been amazing, filled with fun, and their house was filled with souvenirs and family photos.

Her mother's photos had pride of place on the mantelpiece and every day she thought of her. She would have been so happy with how things had turned out. Annabel liked to think that she was looking down on them, content and thrilled that Aidan had two parents who loved him dearly, a tribe of people who would all drop everything to come to his aid.

Tom and Lloyd were blissfully happy too, their dream of becoming a family finally a reality. They were back in London, no doubt run ragged by their very cute and very active twin boys, Jayden and Nathan. When they'd first gone round to see them at their house she'd caught Harry looking at her more than a few times, not that he didn't anyway. He was always finding excuses to touch her, always looking her way, as though he thought she might just vanish in a puff of smoke. This time was different though; these looks were ones of concern. She was rolling around on the floor, tickling the twins while Aidan pretended that the floor was lava, making them gurgle with delight. He needn't have worried though, and she'd told him as much that night. Whilst she loved being auntie to the gorgeous boys, she was just as glad to hand them back.

She remembered all too well how hard it had been raising baby Aidan, and their lives together had so many more things in it. Travel, their jobs, watching their son grow into a fine young man. Harry had even persuaded her to buy a puppy and, given the space they now had at home, she had finally relented. They were picking a rescue puppy up from the local shelter on their return; they'd had a pregnant Labrador bitch come in and the pups would be ready for new homes a few days after they returned home from their trip. Aidan had no idea; she couldn't wait to see his face when they went to collect him. Another boy in the household to love.

The four of them were so happy together, Abe keeping well, still as moody as ever. He was getting ready to retire, his practice safe in the hands of a doctor he'd recruited and trained up. Well, doggedly nagged at more like. The man was nothing short of a stickler, but he was far less sour these days. Having his son back and his fractured family back together suited him well. Harry and he were closer than ever, always laughing and discussing medical journals and breakthroughs together. They saw the merits of each profession and regaled each other with stories of great saves and low moments. There wasn't anything they wouldn't do for the little man in their lives, and her. Abe had even joined the nagging train about the puppy too, even going as dirty as playing the cholesterol card on her. For weeks before she'd finally given in, he had taken to emailing her medical evidence of how pets helped cognitive function in developing adults, and helped the elderly feel less alone and vulnerable to ill health.

The man would live to be a hundred, and he had more friends than Mark Zuckerberg, but she loved him for it. These Carter men were determined; she knew that only too well.

The three men in her life were about to become four, although she hoped that the four-legged new addition would give her less trouble than the first three. Secretly, she was looking forward to it herself now, and she had a whole army of dog walkers and sitters on hand for when they had to juggle their shifts. She still marvelled to herself at how her life had changed.

'You back?' Harry asked, twirling her around on the spot, pulling her out of her private world once more. 'Where do you go when you do that?' he asked, the love and adoration plain on his face as he pulled her close once more.

'Nowhere far,' she said, a teasing smile on her tired but happy face. 'Just thinking about how things turned out.'

'Hard to believe, isn't it?'

'You're telling me. I wanted to run you over in the car park when I first saw you. Tom saved your life that day, you know.'

Harry laughed as she rested her head on his chest, feeling his heartbeat quicken, the low rumble in his chest.

'I owe Tom a few more babysitting sessions then.'

Harry was a great uncle, equally as great as he was a doting father, son and husband. The three boys all loved him, and he them. It was great to see him with them, and she thanked her lucky stars every single morning she awoke in his arms.

'Ten at the very least; I'm an excellent driver.'

'I'm glad you didn't,' he said earnestly. 'And you're not that great. Our fence post would disagree, I think you'll find.'

'Hey! There was a squirrel there, I told you!'

They laughed together, turning back towards the view and looking out at the landscape laid before them. They were in Dubai together, finally. And now it was all the more special. Because they had finally found each other again, and their family was complete. She couldn't wait to see what the next decade would bring. Something told Mrs Annabel Carter that she wouldn't want to miss one single second of it. Life was for living, and loving, and giving second chances. One call could change a life for ever, and no one knew that better than her.

As they headed to bed much later that evening, lying there in the dark, she sent up a silent prayer of thanks for everything she had.

'I love you,' Harry sighed, pulling her close as they let sleep claim them both.

'I love you too.' She smiled in the darkness, kissing him again. She never wanted to stop kissing this man. And she never did.

* * * * *

LET'S TALK
Romance

For exclusive extracts, competitions
and special offers, find us online:

 facebook.com/millsandboon

 @millsandboonuk

 @millsandboon

Or get in touch on 0844 844 1351*

For all the latest titles coming soon,
visit millsandboon.co.uk/nextmonth

*Calls cost 7p per minute plus your phone company's price per
minute access charge